It was an innocent walk in the woods....

Which had turned into a nightmare!

One moment Georgina was strolling through the leafy bowers, the next she was being snatched away by the notorious Lord Graydon, a man rumored to have murdered his wife and led a life of debauchery ever since.

What would happen to her good name? For to spend one night in the clutches of this disreputable man, no matter that it was against her will, would ruin her chances of a respectable life forever...

...provided, of course she lived to tell the tale!

COME WITH US
ON A JOURNEY TO THE PAST....

As publishers of **Masquerade** Historicals,
we want to take you to the fascinating world of
romance and intrigue in times gone by.

Masquerade Historicals will sweep you
back to a distant day filled with lavish balls and
masked ladies, wicked conspiracies and vicious
highwaymen, a world filled with intrigue and danger...
but most of all with love.

We know you will treasure these very special new
books, for each and every one is a reading experience
you won't forget. Every month new titles are released
and can be found wherever paperback books are sold.

Bon voyage!

Sincerely,

THE PUBLISHERS
Masquerade Historicals

The Abducted Heiress

JASMINE CRESSWELL

A MASQUERADE HISTORICAL FROM

W🌐RLDWIDE

TORONTO • LONDON • NEW YORK

Masquerade Historical edition published May 1980
ISBN 0-373-30041-7

Originally published in 1978
by Robert Hale Limited

Printed in Canada

CHAPTER ONE

L<small>ADY</small> E<small>LIZABETH</small>, fourth baroness of Thayne, adjusted the folds of her satin demi-train and seated herself on a low chair placed conveniently close to the fireside. The large salon was elegantly furnished and newly draped, but still cold in the draughty corners. She took several delicate sips from her wine glass and covertly examined the unprepossessing countenance of her only son. Her eye caught Frederick's vacant gaze as he peered with difficulty over the high points of his collar, and she stifled a sigh. At the same time she managed to convey the impression that she continued to devote the full powers of her concentration to the convolutions of Lord Thayne's agitated conversation. Lady Elizabeth's carefully polite expression successfully concealed intense irritation that was directed in almost equal proportions at her husband and her son. With increased determination Lady Elizabeth fixed the smile on to her lips and wondered, not for the first time, how she had ever managed to marry such an excessively unintelligent man.

Comfortably assured that he commanded his family's full attention, Lord Thayne was well occupied in outpouring a detailed catalogue of his latest grievances. His wife knew better than to interrupt before the real source of his irritation had emerged and her patience was finally rewarded.

"Elizabeth, it's that demmed niece of ours. I told you we should have had her presented when she was eighteen." Lord Thayne sputtered slightly with rage. "I actually heard a couple of fellows talking about her in the club when I was in town yesterday. Dashed impudent upstarts were wondering what had happened to old Richard Thayne's daughter."

Lady Elizabeth remained silent, her expression preoccupied, and Lord Thayne rambled on. "That's the trouble, you know. Richard had a lot of friends and there are too many people who remember he left behind a young daughter. And what's more," he concluded gloomily, "they remember the ridiculous terms of Richard's will." He paused to help himself to a substantial swallow of the wine a footman had poured into his glass and then stared moodily into its depths. "Nobody remarked on the girl's absence from town for a couple of seasons, but there are too many cursed gossips with long memories and nothing better to do than rake over old scandals. Now people are beginning to make calculations and to remind themselves that I have a niece who's an heiress, who's pushing twenty-two years old, and has never been seen in town." Angrily he turned to his son. "I won't have it any longer. This is my final word. You're to marry the girl and that'll end the matter."

Frederick Thayne, not noted for his brains but well-endowed with an obstinacy fostered by years of parental over-indulgence, banged down his glass on a marble table and stamped his foot with a petulance singularly reminiscent of the nursery.

"I won't. I tell you I wouldn't marry that fish-faced cousin of mine if she was the last female left in town. Mamma, speak to Papa for me. Tell him that I cannot be expected to subject myself to matrimony with that dowdy . . . that half-wit!"

Lady Elizabeth placed a soothing hand upon her son's arm, gently forcing him back down into his seat upon the sofa. Quietly she turned again to face her husband.

"Tell me, Thayne, have we only club gossip to contend with, or are there other, more serious matters?"

Lord Thayne shifted uncomfortably and thrust his glass out to the silent footman. He avoided his wife's gaze as he spoke.

"Viscount Benham is back in town from Vienna. As the other trustee of my brother's will he naturally found several matters to discuss with me. He took it upon himself to comment at length on the fact that my niece's income has been routinely overspent without any apparent benefit accruing to my niece. Benham was . . . insulting . . . in his insinuations to say the least."

Lady Elizabeth spoke softly. "You explained to him, of course, about the volatile state of Georgiana's nerves? About her childish disposition? About the need for rest and quiet?"

"I expounded on them all at considerable length, I can assure you. Hinted that we were only waiting for her . . . maturity . . . to increase before announcing her engagement to Freddie. Can't say Benham was delighted at the match, but he seemed to accept my word that a season in town would have been too much for the girl."

Lord Thayne tossed the remainder of his wine down his throat and turned belligerently to his son. "Benham's coming down on a visit next week and he expects to find you here, dancing attendance on your cousin. Once he arrives, I shall tell him that your betrothal will be announced at a family dinner party next month. That should take his mind off financial matters that need not concern him. And you make sure that you act the love-sick suitor, my boy, while he's with us. Once he's gone and you're safely married to Georgiana, as far as I'm concerned you need never speak to her again. Put her in a little house on the estate and take off for London. But you're marrying her, do you hear? And that's my last word on the subject."

Recognising the fatal stubbornness of the weak-minded, Lady Elizabeth allowed her cool voice to override Freddie's petulant protest. "Well, Thayne, I shall take pleasure in making Viscount Benham's stay enjoyable for him." She glanced significantly towards the silent footmen. Lady Elizabeth was too astute to make the common mistake of ignoring the presence of family servants. "Perhaps we could discuss our arrangements for Viscount Benham's visit during dinner? And, Frederick," she turned to her son, "you might like to leave us after we have eaten so that your father and I may consider what had best be done about dear Georgiana. It seems to me that there are many matters to be taken into account here, and we must not let your father's excellent judgment be overtaken by any dubious need for haste." She managed to produce a patient smile for Lord Thayne.

"Perhaps, my love, you might care to discuss some alternative plans with me and I will do my best to advise you. Of course, I realise that I cannot bring to bear such wide experience as you, with your great understanding of the world, but I will try to see if there is any little idea that I might contribute."

Lord Thayne puffed out his chest and looked suddenly happier. He made a somewhat half-hearted disclaimer in response to his wife's praise and followed her with docile steps to the dining-room table. The family party was in the process of seating itself around this vast expanse of polished wood when Freddie remarked somewhat testily, "We've forgotten to send for Georgie."

Lady Elizabeth permitted a brief exclamation of annoyance to escape her well-bred lips. She spoke to the butler. "Please see that Miss Thayne is told that we are ready to dine."

"Very good m'lady. I believe Miss Thayne was last seen in the library." The butler moved quietly to the doors and spoke briefly to the footman stationed in the massive hall.

Lady Elizabeth's carefully controlled expression finally registered a modicum of impatience. "You may commence serving, Johnson. Miss Thayne will no doubt be with us very shortly."

Serving of the first course was, in fact, well advanced when the footman opened the dining room doors and the depressingly ungainly Miss Thayne attempted to make an inconspicuous entry to the dinner table. Johnson, the butler, pulled out her chair in silent sympathy as she murmured a vague apology for her late appearance. Lord Thayne, Lady Elizabeth and Frederick acknowledged her presence with barely adequate courtesy, and continued their conversation exactly as if no interruption had occurred.

Georgiana Thayne seemed to suffer no particular pangs at her exclusion from the desultory exchange of family news which constituted the staple ingredient in the talk around the table. She selected a variety of food from the platters offered to her and ate her way through the contents of her plate in stolid silence. She had

quietly refused all offers of creams, jellies and sweet-
meats and was sipping her wine with a notable lack of
enthusiasm, when her uncle suddenly directed a
slightly drunken glance in her direction.

"Well Georgiana," he remarked with hearty jovial-
ity, "we have just been making some exciting plans for
your future."

Lady Elizabeth cast an anguished look in her husband's direction, but Lord Thayne was by now far too
mellowed by wine to pay heed to silent wifely admoni-
tions. Georgiana's expression remained characteristi-
cally bovine, but her long and surprisingly elegant
fingers tightened slightly around the stem of her
wineglass.

"Yes, Uncle William?" Georgiana's voice was high
and unnaturally child-like for a girl who was clearly past
the first bloom of youthfulness. Lord Thayne, flushed
with the confidence endowed by a full bottle of wine
and several brandies, allowed neither his wife nor his
son to speak.

"Yes, Georgiana," he repeated, "we have decided
that Frederick can wait no longer for the pleasure of
making you his bride. The betrothal will be announced
next month." Forgetful of his audience he added, "That
ought to stave Benham off for a while."

Frederick could contain his displeasure no longer.
"Oh I say, sir, we agreed nothing. Mamma . . ." In vain
he looked towards Lady Elizabeth who seemed determined for the moment to take no part in the conversation.

Georgiana appeared momentarily white-cheeked,
but no doubt felt overpowered by the excitement of her
uncle's announcement, for she clapped her hands
together with girlish enthusiasm and turned her smiles

upon her cousin. "Oh, Frederick, how exciting! We shall soon be married and I shall come with you to London and be with you *all* the time. How happy we shall be together!"

Frederick, rendered less articulate than usual by the visions set in train by his cousin's remarks, stuttered over his dessert and glowered silently at his father. Georgiana, the picture of childish delight, puffed out her round cheeks and continued to pour forth trivialities expressing her delight at the sudden change in her immediate prospects. Lord Thayne glared at his son and patted Georgiana's arm approvingly.

"You've always been a good girl, Georgie," he said. "Not your fault you've no brains and no looks. Always said your father should never have married a bluestocking. But there, he would marry a woman with too much education and you're the result. Your mamma's brains all got used up in book-learning and there was nothing left for you."

Georgiana nodded her head in sad agreement, but did venture a small protest. "Mamma was very beautiful, too," she said quietly, her voice suddenly lower and less childish.

Lady Elizabeth looked up sharply from her dissection of a hothouse peach, but Georgiana's face revealed only the expected emotions of uncomplicated pleasure, and Lady Elizabeth contented herself with remarking, "You will enjoy coming with me to choose some lengths of silk for your new clothes. I expect we shall be entertaining many members of the family over the next several weeks."

Georgiana's hands moved restlessly among the pieces of table silver by her plate. "Will my godfather be coming to see us?" she enquired of the table at large.

There was a small silence and Georgiana rushed into it. "I have my new horse to show him, and I know he will be interested in Queenie's latest litter of puppies. You will remember that he gave me Queenie before he left for Vienna."

Lady Elizabeth answered repressively, "Viscount Benham will be honouring us with a visit some time next week." As if conscious of having spoken too much, Georgiana retreated into her former silence and made no further effort to participate in the talk around the table. It was therefore with a feeling of surprise that she realised some minutes later that the meal was finally drawing to a close, and that her aunt was addressing her in tones of determined patience.

Georgiana spoke contritely. "I'm sorry, Aunt Elizabeth. I'm afraid I was not attending."

Lady Elizabeth sighed and repeated her remarks. "I said, Georgiana, that you and I will not withdraw as we usually do, since I am sure Frederick has much that he would like to discuss with you. You may proceed into the small salon and your uncle and I will join you both very shortly."

Georgiana nodded meekly and Lady Elizabeth reflected silently and somewhat scornfully that she need worry about no improprieties where her niece and Frederick were concerned. Although Frederick was her own son, she was unable to quell the thought that his bride-to-be was just about all he deserved in looks and in intellect. Lady Elizabeth allowed herself to wonder why the malignant fates invariably bestowed huge fortunes on females such as Georgiana and left capable women such as herself at the mercy of the first man who cared to offer for them. Looking at Georgiana's simpering expression and unattractive features, Lady

Elizabeth could not prevent herself visualising the probable appearance of her grandchildren, and she shuddered.

Frederick rose to his feet and with ill grace assisted Georgiana to rise from her chair, draping lace shawls around her shapeless figure with evident distaste. He was not himself blessed with perfect discrimination and colour sense, but even he realised that Georgiana's outfit was appallingly ill-chosen. The dress was white as became a young unmarried woman, but her shawls and trimmings each seemed to be in a different inappropriate shade of pink. Georgiana's hair, he noticed for the first time, was a remarkable yellow-gold, but since her eyelashes were fair, her face curiously paunchy, and her skin unattractively red across the high cheekbones, Freddie could be forgiven for thinking that his cousin could not have looked less attractive even if she had tried.

Apparently unaware of her cousin's train of thought, Georgiana prattled happily and inanely as they left the dining room and proceeded into the salon, her childish treble floating back to Lord Thayne and Lady Elizabeth who remained seated at the table.

Once in the salon, however, she seemed overcome by nervousness and fell uneasily silent. Freddie, thinking longingly of London and the raven-haired ballerina who currently enjoyed his patronage, wondered if *any* marriage settlement could make life with Georgiana worthwhile. Georgiana took a deep breath and turned unexpectedly swiftly to face her betrothed.

"Do you really want to marry me, Frederick?" Her cousin was too startled to think up any acceptable reply, and certainly too startled to notice the subtle change in Georgiana's voice and manner. He mumbled a few platitudinous phrases of which "honour" "happy" and "settlements" were the only audible words.

"Do you need money yourself, Freddie, or is it just my uncle?" asked Georgiana, but her cousin turned to her, genuine astonishment mingling with his evident dislike of the question.

"Not at all the thing to discuss the settlements with me, Georgie. That'll all be done with m'father and with Viscount Benham I dare say. No females understand money, not even the clever ones, so you don't want to bother *your* head trying to unravel problems that are above you." He patted her cheek patronisingly. "Don't worry. I'll see that you have plenty of funds to keep your wardrobe up-to-date, and to buy all the trinkets you women seem to like." Despairingly he re-examined his cousin and thought silently that never would good sterling have been so vainly spent.

Georgiana shrugged and Freddie wondered what strange thoughts were troubling her somewhat inadequate wits. Her mood was now changed once again, and with appalling gaucheness she bustled up to him and remarked confidingly, "You may kiss me now, Freddie, for we are to be married very soon, after all."

She screwed her lips up into a tight ball, and thrust her face close to Freddie's. Since Georgiana was rather tall and Freddie was regrettably short, their eyes were almost level and Freddie found himself staring with hypnotised horror into a pair of enormous and expressionless blue eyes. Her pale lashes fluttered down on to her unfashionably red cheeks, and Freddie managed to brush his lips across Georgiana's brow. He hoped that she did not feel the faint shudder of revulsion that could not altogether be repressed. His hands were resting on the shawls draping Georgiana's arms, and he noticed a slight tremor that ran through his cousin as she removed herself to the opposite side of the room. To his very great relief they were spared the effort of further conversation as Lord and Lady Thayne entered the room.

The tea-tray was brought in shortly thereafter, and the rest of the evening passed off in patterns of boring familiarity. Only Lady Elizabeth's parting reminder that Georgiana should be ready in the morning to journey to the cloth merchant in Bristol, indicated that this was indeed an evening out of the ordinary run.

CHAPTER TWO

THE carriage had been waiting for some time at the front door and the coachman was beginning to look anxious. The carriage horses were finely bred and sensitive to the chill easterly wind blowing across from the Cotswolds. Inside the great hall, Lady Elizabeth paced up and down, making no effort to conceal her extreme annoyance.

The housekeeper and the butler, hurrying back from their separate searches, appeared in the hallway together but both were forced to confess failure. Mrs. Bridges had found no trace of Miss Thayne either in her bedchamber or in any of the private sitting-rooms upstairs, nor had Miss Thayne left word of her whereabouts with any of the maids. Johnson was similarly lacking in useful information. Miss Thayne had been seen leaving the house early that morning by a wandering kitchen-boy. Nobody had seen her since.

Having delivered their messages, both servants looked sympathetically at their mistress. Miss Thayne was notorious for her absent-mindedness, although Johnson thought privately that any young lady who could forget an appointment to buy wedding clothes had to be a bit wanting in her wits. It was true that Miss Thayne was as good-natured as a young lady could possibly be, but nobody could deny that her vagueness and irresponsibility rendered her a sad trial to her strong-minded aunt.

Lady Elizabeth pulled her gloves on with a decided snap and spoke curtly to the housekeeper. "It's too late to change my plans now, since I have sent word to the cloth merchants that I am coming today to make my selection. I shall proceed to Bristol as I planned and choose whatever is necessary for Miss Thayne. Please ask her to wait for me in my sitting-room, once she returns."

Mrs. Bridges murmured a suitably subdued "Yes m'lady," but did feel a slight surge of sympathy for the errant Miss Thayne. Lady Elizabeth's anger was awesome and all the more frightening because it was invariably quiet and entirely controlled. However, Miss Thayne never appeared noticeably perturbed on the frequent occasions that she incurred her aunt's displeasure, and Mrs. Bridges had long ago decided that poor Miss Thayne's feeble intellect was a blessing that enabled her to survive many an emotional storm that would have wrecked a more sensitive constitution. If only the poor young lady were a little more attractive, she would no doubt have been the perfect wife for any dashing young aristocrat anxious to ally himself with noble blood and inherited wealth, without acquiring the inconvenience of a wife who demanded constant attention.

Lady Elizabeth seated herself inside the carriage with an impatient swirl of velvet, and the coachman was happy to allow the restless horses to set a brisk pace down the carriageway and on to the lane. The coach disappeared around a curved sweep of highway and the Thayne household resumed its morning duties.

Georgiana waited until all sounds from the carriage

had faded into the far distance and then emerged from the convenient thickness of the shrubbery which had served to conceal her from searching eyes. Her dress, of pale blue muslin, became her rather better than the unfortunate pinks of the previous evening, but its thin fabric could not hope to conceal Georgiana's bulky figure, and its sash sat somewhat uncomfortably upon a non-existent waist. Georgiana removed several burrs of grass from the hem of her gown, tightened the straps of her walking pattens, and set off down the carriageway. Shrubs and trees formed a border for most of its length, and she had to trust that these would provide an adequate screen should anybody chance to look out from the house. Thayne Hall was situated more than three miles from the village of Thayne, and Georgiana wished that she could have taken the short cut to the village across the fields. Heavy rain in the night rendered such a scheme hopelessly impractical, however, and she resigned herself to a long but not unpleasant walk in the wake of her aunt's carriage.

The three miles to the village were accomplished without incident, and Georgiana spent so much of the distance lost in her own thoughts that the beauty of an early spring day was quite lost on her. She reached the tiny house that was her destination and turned into the short entrance path with a slight relaxation in her general air of vague abstraction. A young serving-girl answered her knock at the door and greeted her cheerfully.

"Why Miss, you're welcome I'm sure. Miss Harris was saying only yesterday as how we haven't seen you here in a long while. If you'd care to come into the parlour, I'll bring you some ratafia while you wait for Miss Harris to get back from her lessons. She'll be here directly."

"Thank you, Mary. Some milk would be welcome if you have it. I'm afraid I neglected to have breakfast before I came out."

Mary was instantly all solicitude, and Georgiana allowed herself to be ushered into the parlour and eased into the room's most comfortable armchair. Her glass of milk and her former governess arrived in the parlour almost simultaneously, and Georgiana felt a lessening of the knots of tension just by looking at the clear eyes and welcoming expression of her old companion.

Georgiana rose politely to her feet. "How do you do, Miss Harris?" she said. "You see that I have come to interrupt your luncheon and to beg for a little advice."

"Georgiana, my dear, you know how pleased I always am to see you. If we proceed at once into the dining-parlour, Mary will bring us some fruit and cakes. Then we shall be able to have a comfortable gossip before I return to my reluctant pupils."

Georgiana smiled, her eyes lighting up with inner laughter. "I gather your latest set of young ladies is still finding the refinements of French verbs a mysterious topic quite unworthy of their attentions?"

Miss Harris sighed. "You know very well, Georgiana, that I teach because it usually gives me pleasure. Thanks to your father's generosity, teaching is not an economic necessity for me. Selina and Edwina are sensible girls, but their father is a farmer, albeit an exceedingly prosperous one, and his daughters know that they are destined to marry farmers. Their parents may have ambitions that seem beyond their allotted station in life, but my pupils have the commonsense of youth and realise only too clearly that an ability to converse in French will prove of no practical use in the lives our society has mapped out for them. However," Miss

Harris's expression brightened, "our lessons have improved recently. I have discovered a pattern book, fresh from Paris, full of elaborate descriptions and written entirely in French. At last Edwina has perceived the usefulness of my knowledge. Even Selina is impressed that I can rattle off itemised translations of button-styles and trims, types of fabric and other equally important matters – all without recourse to my phrasebook! So, with frequent relaxations among the fashion plates we have finally managed to struggle through the first quarter of our irregular French verbs."

Miss Harris smiled somewhat ruefully at Georgiana, sat down at the small dining table and indicated the chair to her right. "Mary will bring in our luncheon shortly," she said, "then we shall be quite alone. But just now you must tell me what you think of these new table-napkins I have recently finished embroidering. I confess to being rather proud of the design."

Georgiana admired the exquisite handwork which Miss Harris was displaying for her approval. She felt unable to contribute much to the conversation herself, and she was grateful to her former governess for the gentle flow of undemanding chatter. Eventually the serving dishes were arranged on the table to Mary's satisfaction, and the serving-girl withdrew. Miss Harris interrupted herself almost in mid-sentence and remarked casually, "You may speak quite freely now, Georgiana. I fear that you must have bad news for me?"

All lingering traces of vapidity were erased from Georgiana's expression. Her voice was clear and pleasantly modulated as she spoke to her governess, although it was impossible to disguise the slight tremor of panic that lay just below the surface of the quiet words.

"I'm afraid that the announcement of my betrothal is going to take place shortly. My uncle's financial straits must be worse than we had suspected. I have so hoped – prayed – that his obsession with the gaming tables might lead to an improvement in his fortunes, but it seems clear that my marriage to Freddie is now his only hope of financial rescue. Certainly he cannot expect to pretend that Freddie is eagerly anticipating our marriage." A wry smile lightened Georgiana's troubled features for a moment. "In fact, my uncle's announcement of my cousin's suit nearly precipitated a social catastrophe. It would be difficult to decide who was more distraught last evening, Freddie or myself."

Miss Harris smiled comfortingly at her former pupil. "No doubt you concealed your feelings rather better than young Mr. Thayne! You have the advantage in several years of practice at dissembling. How I wish that such deceit were no longer necessary!" Miss Harris fell into silent thought for a few minutes. "We know that Viscount Benham is back in London, and I think we must rest our hopes upon his intervention. His secretary wrote to me this week and indicated that the Viscount would make all possible speed to come and visit your uncle's household here in the country. I suppose we should try and console ourselves by reflecting that we are lucky you have been able to hold Cousin Freddie at bay for so long."

Georgiana answered gratefully, "Yes, I gathered that Viscount Benham would be visiting us shortly, and of course I'm indebted to you for alerting him to the possible . . . difficulties . . . of my situation."

Georgiana toyed with a minute portion of chicken on

her plate. "I can never thank you sufficiently, Miss Harris, for undertaking to write to my godfather on my behalf. Since my aunt takes it upon herself to read all my letters before they are delivered to the mail, I have often wondered what my godfather must think of the girlish effusions he receives from me. The enthusiastic outpourings over the merits of my latest horse must sound rather peculiar to a man who surely ought to recall how different my interests were when he knew me as a young girl."

Miss Harris considered Georgiana's remarks. "I have often wondered why Viscount Benham took no note of the difficulties which you have experienced since your father died. Seven years is a long time for a trustee to resign all direct supervision of an estate – especially one which is as large as yours. However, we have to remember that your godfather has been engaged in almost ceaseless diplomatic negotiations with France, and then he has assumed the burden of representing our government at the Congress of Vienna, so it is perhaps not to be wondered at if he has had no time for observing the strangeness of your correspondence."

Georgiana assented gloomily. "Miss Harris, I am so afraid that we may be refining too much upon my godfather's support. It is true that he will be aghast at the misappropriation of funds that has occurred. Nevertheless, I believe that my uncle has kept the landed property in admirable condition since he is a true farmer at heart and my aunt is a talented and economical domestic manager. *We* see that marriage between Freddie and myself would be insupportable, that I would be left to a life of penury and obscurity while my cousin and my uncle gambled and . . . and . . . caroused in London. But I fear Viscount Benham may see the marriage as nothing more than a logical union of my fortune and Frederick's future title."

Miserably Georgiana glanced at her chicken, still lying uneaten on her plate. "After all, Miss Harris, had my father not died so unexpectedly he would probably have remarried and produced a male heir. In which case my fortune would have been considerably less, and my matrimonial prospects less bright. Viscount Benham is very much a man of the world. He will probably consider a moronic and unloving husband a small price to pay in return for achieving security, the prospect of a title, and a sensible disposition of my fortune that will preclude the fearful possibility of a family scandal."

Miss Harris spoke sharply. "Georgiana, you are allowing yourself to be depressed by the events of yesterday evening. We cannot pretend that a forced betrothal to your cousin is unexpected, although we may regret that it is being urged upon you precisely at the moment when we hoped that your masquerade had achieved its objective. But we must not be discouraged." She smiled mischievously at her former charge. "When I look at your present appearance, I cannot think that Freddie will ever become an earnest supporter of his father's schemes. We know Viscount Benham to be an enlightened and considerate man, so we must hope that he can be brought to understand your aversion to the betrothal. It is not unreasonable, especially by the standards of your godfather's social world, for a young lady to expect a season in London before settling down to the supposed joys of wedded bliss."

Georgiana laughed at last. "I see you are still an Unbeliever, dear Harry!" Miss Harris tried unsuccessfully to look reproving at the use of the childish nickname. Georgiana spoke more seriously. "You may safely disparage the male sex and the dubious benefits of matrimony, but since I have no choice other than to marry, you must allow me the comfort of my romantic dreams. Surely in the whole of England there must be one or two gentlemen of kindly disposition who are willing to believe that a mere female may have worthwhile ideas on some subjects other than household routines and feminine apparel?"

Miss Harris took Georgiana's slim white hand within her clasp and patted it gently. "Indeed, I'm sure that there are several gentlemen who would appreciate your true worth, Georgiana. Our only problem is finding out how we may contrive to have you meet these paragons. Lady Elizabeth, your aunt, is possessed of a sharp mind. She has perceived quite clearly that she need take no desperate measures to keep your fortune hidden from the world. She needs only to deny you the opportunity of a season at London, or at one of the lesser gathering places of the *ton*, and your fortune is safely reserved to Freddie. There are no eligible bachelors in the immediate neighborhood – and how else is anybody to meet you here?"

Georgiana made a small and unladylike grimace. "Looking as I do, it is not very probable that any casual visitor, even if my aunt had any, is likely to be bowled over by my feminine charms. I am beginning to wonder if the disadvantages my appearance entails now warrant . . . Why, Mary," suddenly Georgiana's voice was higher pitched and subtly childish. "Have you come to tell me I must depart and leave your mistress free to return to her duties?"

"Oh no, not really, Miss Thayne. Except, well, maybe I thought as how I should remind Miss Harris of the time. But if you haven't finished your lunch I'll just go away again."

Georgiana rose to her feet before Miss Harris was able to reply. "I have to return home now, anyway." She smiled a little vacantly at Miss Harris. "The vicar and his wife will be eating dinner with us this Sunday after Church. I do hope you will join us as usual."

Miss Harris nodded a formal assent. Sunday dinners at Thayne Hall were an established part of her weekly routine. Since the vicar had been appointed for his skills in the hunting field rather than for his skills in the pulpit or as a rational conversationalist, she found the lengthy dinners somewhat of an ordeal. However, Georgiana relied on her presence and they usually managed to enjoy an hour of one another's company when the remainder of the party retired to sleep off the effects of over-indulgence at the table.

Miss Harris suppressed a sigh as she escorted Georgiana into the tiny entrance hall of the cottage. For a girl who was not physically imprisoned, Georgiana was almost unbelievably isolated from potential friends and companions. Social barriers successfully prevented intimacy with the good-natured daughters of the village apothecary and the village notary. The local squire was elderly and cared for by a devoted spinster sister who extended punctilious courtesy but no warmth to Georgiana. Graydon Place, the only other great house in the neighbourhood, remained unoccupied, its tenant farms falling into gradual and depressing decline.

That house was, in fact, shrouded in the delicious remnants of a mysterious scandal that had shattered local sensibilities at least six years earlier. Its owner, the Marquis of Graydon, was an acknowledged rake whose libertine propensities seemed to become magnified with each retelling of his wild career. Local society drew a discreet and rather bewildering veil over the exact nature of his crimes, but it did seem certain that having driven his poor wife out of the house by his terrible behaviour, he had challenged her lover to an unfair duel and killed his unfortunate bride when she attempted to prevent the unseemly shooting match. Georgiana could not help feeling that a wife with an acknowledged lover could not be considered altogether blameless in the affair, but it was generally held to be fortunate that the Marquis had taken the shattered remnants of his fortune and reputation off to foreign parts, for he would certainly never again be received in the neighbourhood.

Miss Harris and Georgiana had often beguiled boring afternoons by investing the absent Marquis with innumerable wicked but fascinating characteristics, vices all the more entrancing for being utterly beyond the narrow experience of either Miss Harris or her pupil. Unfortunately, the absent villain remained permanently absent, thus failing to add fuel to the flickering embers of the dying scandal, and Miss Harris had recently decided that a normal household with cheerful daughters and easy-going sons would be welcome replacements for the second-hand thrills of half-remembered scandal about an unknown Marquis.

She contrived to reveal none of these gloomy reflections as she said an affectionate goodbye to Georgiana. She watched her former pupil's stolid figure walk slowly through the village and wondered for the hundredth time if Georgiana was correct in maintaining her role as the slow-witted but entirely dutiful niece of Thayne Manor. Georgiana was convinced that any show of resistance to her aunt's iron will would result in a total loss of freedom. She repeatedly assured Miss Harris that she needed to feign stupidity and docile willingness in almost equal proportions. By these methods Georgiana had successfully contrived to remain largely forgotten within the walls of Thayne Hall, rarely coming in contact either with her cousin or her compulsively gambling uncle who naturally preferred the joys of the London tables to the tame round of country hospitality. So for close to six years, burdened with the excessive fortune bestowed on her by two adoring parents, she had staved off matrimony with her impoverished cousin and escaped most of the serious backlash of her aunt's cold temper. But the price her pupil paid had always been heavy, and Miss Harris knew that the moment was surely approaching when some confrontation with Lord and Lady Thayne would have to occur.

With a sudden return to realisation of her whereabouts, Miss Harris recognised that Mary had been waiting patiently for some time, holding out a bonnet, mittens and a small parasol although the sun was not particularly strong this early in the year. She smiled her thanks at the maid, swiftly tied the strings of her bonnet and set off for the vicarage where her assortment of young ladies would doubtless be happy to note the lateness of her arrival. Although her mind was already busy with plans for the afternoon's lessons – she took her duties as a teacher extremely conscientiously – Miss Harris allowed herself time to hope that Viscount Benham would arrive *very* soon.

CHAPTER
THREE

GEORGIANA sat in front of the dressing-room mirror, her hands shuffling idly among the items in her trinket-box as she tried to consider dispassionately what course of action she ought to follow. Viscount Benham had arrived before noon and had spent the afternoon closeted with her uncle in the library. Georgiana waited hopefully, but no opportunity to see her godfather had arisen, and it was becoming increasingly clear that her godfather's visit might come and go before she ever managed to speak to him alone and at any length.

Lady Elizabeth harboured no deep suspicions concerning the true nature of her niece's character and intellect, but she was too wily a campaigner to permit any potentially embarrassing contact between Georgiana and Viscount Benham if it could be avoided. Sitting regally behind the afternoon tea-tray, Lady Elizabeth had taken the opportunity to expound on the correct behaviour of a dutiful niece, and Georgiana had been left in no doubt as to the way in which she was expected to conduct herself when the meeting with Viscount Benham finally occurred. Lady Elizabeth spoke of the betrothal as an established fact that had already received her godfather's blessing, and Georgiana could only reflect miserably that her behaviour the evening before had given her aunt every justification for expecting her niece's full co-operation in hastening the betrothal to its logical conclusion.

At this precise moment Georgiana had also to face up to the dilemma created by the strange appearance and infantile manner she habitually adopted within the family circle. On the one hand she could not effect too drastic a change for fear of arousing the curiosity of all the guests at dinner. On the other hand, she could not afford to appear as appallingly badly dressed as usual, or her godfather, even if he still retained any interest in her future, might find himself prejudiced against her pleas for assistance.

Stirred to action by the lateness of the hour, Georginia selected a plain white gown of fine lawn and added a knitted stole ready to drape around her shoulders. The large salons of Thayne Hall had been designed for elegance rather than for warmth or comfort, and Georgiana had learned to use the chilly draughts of air as an excuse to bury the smooth line of her shoulders and conceal the slender column of her neck beneath a huddled bundle of woollen draperies.

It was several years now since Georgiana had accepted more than superficial help with her toilette. Hooks and buttons were of necessity fastened by a maid, but Georgiana took care to select clothing that she could don virtually unaided. Fortunately, Lady Elizabeth was rigorously economical in managing the household and Georgiana was expected to make do with whatever time Lady Elizabeth's maid could spare. Since Marguerite was blessed with a snobbish spirit that almost exceeded Lady Elizabeth's own, Georgiana was usually able to scramble through the brief periods she spent enduring Marguerite's ministrations in an obsequious and bumbling silence.

Even so, Marguerite had the acute eye of a highly trained dresser, and Georgiana was never entirely easy until the nightly ordeal with Marguerite was safely past. Tonight her concern was greater than usual. Her face was, as usual, oddly puffed out and ugly around the cheeks and her figure as bulky as ever. But the simple lines of her dress highlighted the attractive colour and texture of her golden hair, her eyes seemed startlingly blue when contrasted with the monochrome whiteness of her clothing, and whereas the pinks she habitually affected made the colour in her cheeks appear excissively hectic, tonight her complexion seemed no more than a pleasing contrast between white forehead and naturally red lips.

Georgiana scowled into the mirror. Marguerite was an artist at heart and there was a grave danger that she might feel inspired by Georgiana's vastly improved looks. If the maid attempted a new and more flattering hair-style, smoothing hair away from the back of Georgiana's neck to reveal the perfection of line, tidying up the frizzy mass of curls framing her face, Georgiana might find the careful planning of the past six years laid waste in a single night. Sighing, Georgiana braced herself for Marguerite's entry and moved, without much hope, into a more shadowy corner of the room.

In the event, her anxieties proved without foundation. Lady Elizabeth was entertaining her visitor with the most elaborate dinner she could command. The squire and his sister, the vicar and his wife, and even some more distant neighbours, were all expected as guests. Marguerite was flooded with requests for assistance and felt nothing but relief when she discovered Miss Thayne dressed and waiting as quietly and as patiently as ever. Silently Marguerite blessed all members of the aristocracy who were dim-witted and even-tempered. She flicked expert fingers over the buttons fastening the back of Miss Thayne's gown, she helped place a tortoishell comb in the back of Miss Thanye's usual hairstyle, and fled to more demanding ladies at the earliest opportunity.

Georgiana slipped into the salon at the latest moment courtesy permitted, reflecting wryly that a reputation for absent-mindedness had its advantages. Lord Thayne and Lady Elizabeth were at the centre of a group of guests, talking politely with Viscount Benham. Freddie had not yet put in an appearance, but the squire and his sister Miss Pemberton were already ensconced on a fireside sofa. The vicar and his lady in turn smiled a patronising welcome to Georgiana, indicated with tepid good manners that she should come and find a place on their side of the great fireplace. Georgiana's progress, however, was halted by Lady Elizabeth, who swept across the room, the satisfaction of a successful hostess writ largely upon her face.

"Dear Georgiana." She permitted herself a fond, almost maternal smile. "Your godfather has been eagerly awaiting your arrival. Such *interesting* news as we have had to tell him!" She smiled archly at the vicar and Mrs. Adams. "But we mustn't reveal our happy family secrets until the proper moment. I must take Georgiana away from you for a short while so that she may become re-acquainted with her godfather. Such a distinguished man!"

Georgiana attempted a wan smile but thought bitterly that her aunt could not have committed her to the engagement more fully if she had posted the banns of marriage upon the church door. Mrs. Adams had a voracious appetite for news of all sorts and could be relied upon to let the entire country know, in confidence, that Miss Thayne was shortly to be betrothed.

As the seemingly endless dinner progressed, Georgiana allowed feelings of desperation to engulf her for the first time since her parents had died. Apparently well primed by his mother, Freddie now seemed resigned to his fate and spent the whole evening paying obvious and tedious court to Georgiana. She ignored him as much as possible, pretending not to understand at least half of his ponderous compliments, and maintained a deliberate air of polite disinterest when it was impossible to pretend incomprehension. To an accompaniment of arch and far from subtle encouragement pouring from the lips of her aunt and uncle, Georgiana responded miserably to the polite conversation of the highly interested guests. She wished that her general demeanour might indicate the depths of her dislike for Freddie, but her monosyllabic replies merely fixed her in the minds of the assembled company as a delightfully modest and unassuming girl. Long used to dismissing her as "that poor Miss Thayne, such a fortune and no looks", the vicar and the squire were genuinely relieved to see that the local heiress was about to be so comfortably and conventionally bestowed, and the whole affair was made even more interesting since it was not yet openly acknowledged. There was nothing, Georgiana concluded in silent frustration, more likely to guarantee the success of a country dinner party than the half-revelation of a family betrothal.

Viscount Benham's contributions to the conversation were neither arch nor noticeably friendly in return to the sometimes fulsome praise heaped upon him by the assembled company. Nevertheless, when Georgiana was at last able to snatch a few moments' private speech with him in the drawing room after dinner, she felt the waves of incipient panic threaten to engulf her. Viscount Benham was not callous, nor was he blind to Freddie's faults. But he was a busy man involved in the complex administration of a foreign policy that he sometimes felt changed hourly under the conflicting pressures of power changes in the court circle and in Parliament. He vaguely remembered Georgiana as the promising and intelligent daughter of the man who had been his closest friend. Sadly, he reflected that the passage of years had not fulfilled the promise of Georgiana's girlhood beauty. He found her conversation dull, but expected little else from the women assembled at a country dinner.

Viscount Benham's wife, whom he had married from a high sense of duty when he was very young, had conveniently obliged him by expiring in childbirth after producing two healthy sons. His acquaintance with women was now habitually limited to the selection of some tolerably attractive and discreet widow with whom he maintained a half-hearted liaison until the pressure of work or a prolonged absence abroad made the connection too fatiguing to maintain. As a leading member of the peerage, endowed with a comfortable wealth, he had ample opportunity for reinforcing his cynical belief that all women could successfully be bought. It was merely a question of the price they could realistically expect to command in the market place.

Chatting amiably, but with unthinking condescension, to Georgiana, he allowed his mind to assess her worth with a cold objectivity that he did not intend to be either unkind or demeaning. For a girl of her social status and fortune, any connection outside marriage was of course unthinkable. She could almost certainly expect to demand a title from any man aspiring to her hand, since her fortune was lavish rather than genteel, and her birth impeccable.

On the other hand, Viscount Benham's cursory inspection revealed no hidden talents and no extraordinary beauty. She had not offered to sing or to play the harp. She had made no effort to quote Italian verse; nor had she larded her conversation with snippets of French. Viscount Benham was prepared to accept her uncle's flat statement that poor old Georgie was a little slow on the uptake. In the circumstances, and particularly in view of Lord and Lady Thayne's almost inexcusable failure to have their niece presented at the proper age, Viscount Benham felt nothing but relief that his godchild was about to be settled so suitably and with so little effort to himself.

His enthusiasm for the match was increased by the slight feelings of guilt which pricked at his conscience whenever he remembered the laxness of his stewardship as trustee of her estate. The Viscount was well aware that Georgiana's income over the past several years had been diverted into her uncle's coffers, but he also saw that her landed inheritance had been maintained in good heart and it had always seemed to him slightly unreasonable that William Thayne should be expected to keep up the position of fourth Baron when all of the unentailed family properly had been willed to his niece. A marriage between Georgiana and Frederick would reunite very tidily a fortune that had been unfortunately split.

Viscount Benham sighed. He had held the greatest admiration for Georgiana's father, but it was widely acknowledged that the late Baron Thayne's love for his wife and daughter had passed all normal bounds of propriety. Henrietta Thayne had been adored while she lived and idolised after she died. Georgiana had inherited her mother's fortune but not, the Viscount concluded mentally, her mother's looks or her mother's distinctly unfeminine depth of intellect.

Georgiana maintained her part of the aimless conversation with her godfather. His face was fixed in its normal mask of social politeness but nevertheless she was well able to guess at the general trend of some of his thoughts. Suddenly she could contain her frustration no longer. "Sir, I beg your assistance. I long to visit London, and wish you could suggest to me how my objective may be achieved." Once the words were spoken Georgiana felt uncertain, fearful of having revealed too much.

Viscount Benham looked startled, then ill-at-ease. He coughed. "Between us, my dear Georgiana, I am sure there need be no false modesty. I am your trustee as well as your godfather, and naturally Lord Thayne has informed me of the happy agreement which has been reached between your cousin and yourself. Surely, since the betrothal is soon to be a matter of public knowledge, we may expect an early wedding? A few weeks in London could doubtless be arranged as part of the bridal trip?" He looked at her unhappy face with discomfort and irritation, and spoke sharply to cover his sense of betrayal. "It would be more appropriate for you to discuss this with your betrothed, Georgiana. You must learn to look to him for advice and instruction, now. I am no longer to be the arbiter of your destiny."

"I don't want to marry Freddie." Georgiana spoke flatly, all feeling drained from her voice by the deadening weight of despair settling around her.

Viscount Benham looked appalled and searched round the room with a wild glance. His eye lighted upon Lady Elizabeth and a look of immediate and mutual rapport flashed between them. At all costs, Georgiana had to be prevented from making the present situation irretrievable. "My dear Georgiana . . ." Lady Elizabeth was beside them both before the Viscount had time to say any more, her voice raised so that it might carry beyond their immediate group.

"My lord, you must come and talk to Freddie about your experiences in Vienna. He longs to hear details of the Congress from one who played *such* an important role." She turned smoothly to her niece.

"Georgiana, I see that Miss Pemberton seeks a partner at backgammon, perhaps you could oblige her?"

Lady Elizabeth sailed away on a cloud of blue silk and Georgiana, hoping that her white muslin didn't look as limp as she was feeling, was obliged to wend her stolid way across the room to Miss Pemberton and the doubtful delights of the backgammon table.

CHAPTER
FOUR

THE pale golden light of early morning was captured in the unending shower of water spraying out from the fountain, scattering coloured beads of moisture on to the freshly scythed grass. A light breeze stirred the trailing fronds of the willow trees, artfully planted to break up the endless vistas of green lawn.

It was an idyllic scene, but Georgiana walked across the smooth grass surrounding the house, oblivious to her surroundings. It had long been her habit to take solitary walks before the rest of the household stirred into wakefulness and this morning, more than ever, she felt the need for absolute solitude.

Although the grounds of Thayne Hall were extensive, her choice of walks was limited if she required privacy. The land to the east had not yet been successfully drained and in springtime was particularly liable to be muddy underfoot. The main windows of the house looked south and west across the driveway and the vast sweeps of lawn and ornamental gardens. In her constant anxiety to avoid prying eyes, Georgiana usually resisted the enticements of a cunningly concealed folly and an ornamental lake that lay in the far western extremity of the property.

She had no particularly strong reason this morning for hiding the direction of her walk, but from force of habit she wended her way across the more roughly tended garden at the back of the house, breathing a sigh of satisfaction as she reached the outskirts of the small wood that marked the northern boundary of Thayne land.

In the years since her father's death, Georgiana had become accustomed to thinking of herself as an adult. She had been only fifteen when her father succumbed to a sudden and virulent fever. But the enormous size of her fortune, the cold scheming immediately visible in her Aunt Elizabeth's face, the unprepossessing vacuousness of cousin Freddie – then an alarmingly spotty eighteen-year-old – had all helped to accelerate Georgiana's precocious rush to maturity. At fifteen, she seemed to push childhood away in her effort to maintain independence of mind and some small freedom of action.

But now Georgiana realised that until last night she had never wholly put the games of childhood behind her. The ridiculous masquerade, designed to keep Freddie's wandering gaze fixed firmly elsewhere, was a scheme thought up by a child, and enjoyed by Georgiana with a chilld's insouciant love of tricking the adult world. To a certain extent her plans could be said to have achieved their objectives. For six years, with the aid of a carefully cultivated reputation for feeble-mindedness, she had managed to lead pretty much the life she chose without ever needing to engage in battle with her formidable aunt. Now, however, her aunt had decided to take a stand and Georgiana realised that her childish defences were utterly breached. She had no power to resist the authority of her appointed guardians. She had no weapons with which to fight against a marriage and a way of life that was entirely distasteful to her. She had no friends other than Miss Harris, who was able to offer nothing more substantial than advice and comfort. Georgiana bent down to pick a long piece of clover, sucking absently at the sweetness as she walked along. Today the magic of the quiet woods was having no effect upon the burden of her problems.

The wood itself was quite small. Long and narrow, it was well traversed by three or four clearly marked paths, all of which converged at a central clearing happily provided with convenient tree-stumps that made comfortable stools for periods of solitary reflection. Georgiana suspected that the paths were kept in a state of repair by the many village poachers, but since her sympathies lay entirely on the side of the underfed she made no mention of the surprisingly bramble-free condition of woodland paths that had not been officially cleared in years. She had also learned to cultivate a studied deafness to strange noises, and when twigs snapped suddenly in the distance she had developed the habit of humming snatches of any song that came into her mind, thus enabling all unauthorised visitors to the wood to fade away (she hoped with their rabbit) before any embarrassing confrontation could occur.

Today, however, the clearing was reached without incident and perversely Georgiana felt herself missing the pleasant sense of successful defiance. Her moments of rebellion were so few that each one needed to be treasured, and the injustice of her lot was suddenly more than Georgiana felt able to bear. She wanted to scream, cry out, fall on some friendly shoulder and beg for help. There was no one. She thought of her elderly grandmother, ailing and always in pain, cloistered in her house outside Bath. Her mother's brother was married to some minor German princess and seemed to be for ever dashing between his family's estates in Devonshire and his wife's vast, but unprofitable, acres in central Germany.

Tears of bitter frustration refused to be held back any longer. Viciously she kicked the trunk of an ancient oak, left standing at the edge of the clearing. Not surprisingly, her action had little effect upon the tree, but left her foot feeling bruised and uncomfortable. Georgiana sat down on a tree stump and removed her shoe. Of course, her stocking now had a hole in it. Her toe was bleeding and extremely painful.

"You seem to be experiencing some difficulty. May I be of assistance?"

Georgiana was too embarrassed to feel surprised. She allowed her shoe to fall to the ground, and hid her naked toe under the hem of her gown, rearranging her skirt primly about her ankles. Then she turned round to confront the owner of the voice.

The man was standing partially concealed in the shadows of the wood, his clothing dark and not readily distinguishable against the brown background of the trees. To Georgiana's heightened sensibilities he seemed enormous, menacing even, and clearly not one of the friendly villagers caught out on a poaching trip.

"Who are you?" There was no difficulty in making her question sound high and stupid on this occasion, since her voice was cracking with fright. He laughed easily, almost patronisingly, Georgiana thought.

"I might ask you the same question. This is, after all, my land."

"Your land?" Georgiana felt more and more bewildered. "No it's not. It's mine. I mean it belongs to Baron Thayne." Her tendency to forget that the lands of the barony were no longer her property was sometimes embarrassing. To mask her confusion she added quellingly, "I am Miss Thayne. Miss Georgiana Thayne."

"Ah?" He sketched a small, mocking bow that combined elegance and insolence in approximately equal proportions. He spoke gently, apologetically, as though humouring a fractious child. "Despite your impressive credentials, I still believe the land to be mine. However, I am pleased to find you so early in the day, and right at the start of my search for you." He added conversationally, "I have been waiting for an opportunity to meet you, Miss Thayne. I very much regret that I require your presence and I must now ask you to accompany me."

Georgiana looked at the stranger warily, no longer attempting to identify him since she was convinced that she dealt with a madman. Which of the local families, she wondered, normally concealed this terrible burden safely within the walls of their home? Innately kind, although still frightened, she tried to think of some way to reassure and calm the trespasser until his keeper might manage to find him.

"I am not insane, you know." Uncannily he had read her mind. He raised his voice somewhat and called out. "Thomas, I have found the lady. You may come and help me now."

Georgiana sought with terrified eyes for some means of escape as she heard the noisy crunch of twigs underfoot. She knew only too well how isolated these woods were from Thayne Hall, and that no villagers would be so foolish as to show themselves, even if they heard her voice. A short stocky man emerged from the thicket, dangling a length of cloth over one arm. Georgiana turned wildly in the direction of the house, but she had run only a few yards before she was caught by a pair of ruthless hands and held immobilised.

Georgiana found her voice. "There is . . . there must be . . . some mistake. We do not know one another. You can have no reason for : . . for . . . whatever . . ." She swallowed hard. "There can be no reason for whatever you plan to do."

The stranger spoke soothingly, as if to somebody he knew was not very clever. His voice proclaimed him unmistakably a gentleman. "I shall explain to you later, but now I have no time. I cannot run the risk of encountering somebody from the village." He spoke even more gently. "Thomas will not hurt you, but I'm afraid I have to insist upon binding your wrists. The cloth is soft and will not hurt you."

Georgiana found her voice and allowed the scream of terror to ring out. Common thugs, highwaymen, she could have tolerated. But this calm expression of madness terrified her as nothing else could have done. Blindly she struggled, realising the utter futility of fighting against two strong men, but unable to control the instinctive responses of her body. She bit, she clawed, she scratched, but eventually the long cloth was in place, her hands bound firmly in front of her.

"Please do not struggle any further." The hated voice came from behind her. There was a rustle of starched cloth, and Georgiana saw the gentleman's cravat being pulled impatiently from his neck and handed to Thomas. "I had not anticipated such lively resistance," he continued, "I fear that I must insist upon a blindfold."

Georgiana was given no opportunity to protest, and her eyes were soon covered by the layers of white muslin.

"We must walk to the edge of the woods, I have a horse waiting for us there. If you will allow Thomas to take your hands we should be able to proceed quite swiftly."

"My shoe . . ." Georgiana now knew what it felt like to be beyond fear.

"Ah yes. The start of today's miseries for you." Unbelievably his voice seemed to contain a thread of laughter. "Thomas, perhaps you would search for Miss Thayne's shoe? I wish to reach home as swiftly as possible."

"But . . ." Georgiana uttered no more, for she was swung off her feet and found herself resting in a pair of remarkably strong arms. The sensation, particularly since her sight was obliterated by the blindfold, was definitely outside anything in her previous experience.

She felt his warm breath upon her neck as he spoke quietly to her. "We have now reached my horse and Thomas has managed to retrieve your shoe. Thomas!" The voice was momentarily turned from her. "If you will hold Diabolo still whilst I mount, we may then between us be able to lift Miss Thayne on to the horse in front of me. You may also be able to replace her shoe."

"I'm not a sack of vegetables," said Georgiana. "If you would only remove this blindfold I am quite capable of mounting the horse myself."

"You must forgive me, Miss Thayne, if I take leave to doubt that. Your appearance is not . . . athletic . . . and Diabolo is not a cart-horse. It would be safer from all points of view if you retained the blindfold."

It was not possible to argue further. She could smell the horse very close to them both now, and with a single light movement her mad captor released the grip on her arms and sprang into the saddle. Her freedom was short-lived, however, for she immediately felt herself clasped around the waist by two separate pairs of hands.

Even in the stress of the moment she found time to wonder if her secret would be discovered, and then all other thoughts were submerged beneath the indignity of being hauled by two strange men up on to a horse.

At first she held herself rigidly unyielding until she realised that this was only prolonging the comically ungraceful period of her removal from ground to horse. Georgiana, finally mounted and clutching the mane of the wretched Diabolo, was almost glad of the blindfold that spared her the sight of her two captors' expressions.

"We seem to be ready, Thomas." There was no mistaking the hateful undercurrent of laughter in his voice this time. "I had moments when I wondered if all was to be lost because of the absence of a mounting-block."

Georgiana ignored the remark as being beneath contempt. She hunched her shoulders further forward, enduring agonies of discomfort as she attempted to remain seated on the horse without allowing any part of her body to come into contact with the man lolling comfortably behind. How incredibly difficult it was to distinguish one sound from another when all light was cut off. Georgiana listened intently and managed to disentangle the sounds of a second rider mounting upon a second horse. No doubt this was the taciturn Thomas, who so far had not uttered a single word during his master's despicable and incomprehensible actions. Some silent signal apparently passed between Thomas and her captor, who urged his horse into a slow canter with a gentle nudge in the flank.

The horse's pace was firm and even, but Georgiana found herself trembling with fright. A reasonably accomplished horsewoman, she made no claims to extraordinary skill, and now she felt herself to be in imminent and very real danger of sliding off the saddle into an ignominious huddle beneath the horse's hooves. Her hands, hopelessly impeded by the cloth binding them together, searched for some security among the thick strands of Diabolo's mane. Abruptly she was jerked back against the leather jacket of the man riding behind her.

"Come, Miss Thayne. Your maidenly modesty is likely to have us both unseated if you persist in pulling at my horse in that fashion. I must urge you to relax against me, or I fear I shall not be able to support you and restrain my horse should the ground become a little rougher."

Georgiana thrust her chin into the air, ignoring his words, but nevertheless relieved to feel the security of a very substantial pair of shoulders supporting her back. "Why are you doing this?" she asked involuntarily. "You do not sound mad, and yet your actions are those of a man who is out of his wits. Even at this moment I cannot believe that I am here, captive, riding before you. Tell me how I have offended you?"

There was a momentary pause, a slight hesitation before she heard the reply. "This is not the moment for explanations, ma'am. You will be informed more fully of my plans before nightfall."

As if to preclude the possibility of further conversation, he spurred the horse into a canter, leaving Georgiana far too breathless and concerned for her present safety to worry about the mysteries of the future.

They rode at this hectic pace for some half-hour, leaving Georgiana entirely unable to guess their whereabouts at journey's end. They had crossed no bridges in so far as she could tell, and had certainly travelled over no gravelled roads, which led her to suspect that they might have ridden due north. In any case, it seemed there was so little likelihood of escape that the direction of her prison was probably immaterial.

Dismounting proved an easier task than Georgiana had feared. She simply waited until told that Thomas had secured Diabolo's head, and then slid down the horse's flanks into the arms that waited to receive her.

"Surely, sir, I may now expect to have this ridiculous bandage removed from my eyes?" Annoyingly, her voice was not as steady as she would have wished. "I find the darkness . . . oppressive."

"I am sorry" he said. Could she detect a note of genuine regret? "My servant will show you to your chamber and then he will remove the covering from your eyes. I regret that I have to leave you now, but it will be my pleasure to join you for dinner this evening."

"But my family!" Georgiana cried. "Sir, I cannot be absent from my home for an entire day in this fashion. Surely you cannot plan to keep me incarcerated here all day?" Desperation caused Georgiana's voice to rise, and she swallowed hastily making a definite physical effort to quell the mounting panic.

Again that quiet, mocking laugh, quickly smothered. "I'm afraid, Miss Thayne, that my plans are precisely to keep you incarcerated here. I think you should resign yourself to being my . . . guest . . . for several days." The self-confident arms reached out to lead her into the confines of whatever building awaited them.

"No!" Georgiana's calm had finally snapped. "No! I will not go with you." Blindly she pulled herself away from the arms that hardly attempted to restrain her, running madly until stopped by the solid strength of

Thomas's stocky figure. She heard his voice then, warm and accented with the soft sounds of Gloucester-shire.

"I couldn't let you go on running, look, Miss. There's a big wall right ahead of ye. Best go in with the master." Georgiana felt defeat overwhelm her, and wearily she allowed herself to be led inside.

It was such a relief to feel hands untying the cloth covering her eyes that for a moment Georgiana could only welcome the sudden light without attempting to distinguish shapes or to interpret forms. As soon as she regained control of her wits she turned round to face her captors, but the grating of a heavy key in the metal lock warned her that they had already left her alone, the sounds of their exit masked by the opulence of the thick woollen carpet that covered the floor.

Feelings of fatigue and despair again threatened to overwhelm Georgiana until the outrageous luxury of the room's furnishings began to impress itself upon her consciousness. Curiosity overcame fear as she saw that the walls were covered in the most modish of silk hangings and the floor was entirely concealed under an exotic oriental rug in a style made fashionable by the Prince Regent. A very modern bed was draped with shining satin covers in a vulgar shade of bright pink and the ornate gilded furniture was evidently barely used. There were two windows in the room, although light entered only from one, since the second window was securely shuttered on the outside. A swift hope that she might escape via the casement was quickly dashed when Georgiana saw that the bedchamber was at least fifteen feet above the ground and entirely devoid of clinging vines or convenient trees – even if she had felt capable of climbing them.

Georgiana felt the relief flood through her because the room was so much less gruesome than she had feared, but the silence of the house remained absolute and even the luxury of her surroundings could not for long control the depressing direction of her thoughts. On the one hand it seemed utterly useless to speculate upon the intentions of her kidnappers . . . On the other hand it was almost impossible to prevent herself imagining the several horrible fates that might be in store for her.

With reluctance she admitted that part of her fears revolved around the character and intentions of her aunt and uncle. Obviously she had been abducted either by criminals or by madmen, and if her abductors were criminals a handsome reward would undoubtedly be needed to obtain her release. And the grim fact surfaced from Georgiana's chaotic thoughts that she was not at all sure that her aunt and uncle would be willing to pay for her safety. The fortune she possessed represented a temptation even to the most high-minded, and neither her uncle nor her cousin Frederick could be considered particularly nice in their moral scruples. Her aunt was certainly more sensitive to the call of duty, but she had no affection for her niece and Georgiana wryly acknowledged that the prospective rewards of her death would be very great, and the benefits of her continued living very small.

It was at this low point in her reflections that Thomas appeared at the door, bearing a large jug of hot water and a platter provided with a modest selection of bread, fruit and milk. Georgiana disdained acknowledgement of the servant's cheerful words of greeting, but an almost imperceptible lightening of her spirits occurred as she registered Thomas' respectful manner and the welcome presence of the means of refreshment. However, she had no wish to display her relief, so she hunched her shoulders towards the servant and walked angrily towards the window, looking out obstinately over the rather unrewarding vista of trees and tangled undergrowth.

Thomas remained impervious to her lack of response, chattering gently as he arranged the platter to his satisfaction and indicating a bowl in which she might wash her face and hands.

"The master's going to be back nice and early, Miss," he said, "and he would be obliged if you would honour him at dinner. We'll be keeping country hours, so you'll be able to get an early night. Mebbe things will look more cheerful tomorrow."

"I do not wish to dine with your master," said Georgiana. "I shall remain here alone until he releases me. I do not care to consort with either criminals or madmen. Perhaps you do not realise that if your master is a criminal you are risking dire penalties for your service to him and if – as I suspect – he is not fully in possession of his faculties, you do him no kindness by allowing him to pursue his follies."

She paused, but Thomas made no move to speak and resignedly Georgiana shrugged her shoulders. "I see it would be useless to beg for your assistance in finding my way out from here, but you may tell your master that I am not prepared to pander to his strange fancies by dining with him."

"Well, I'll tell him, Miss." Thomas sounded uncertain. "But I don't reckon as how it'll make much difference in the end. Planning this for some months now, he has been." Then, as if conscious of having betrayed more than he ought, he hastily bowed and withdrew, the key grating ominously in the heavy lock.

Georgiana was once more left with little to do but speculate uneasily on her immediate fate and wonder how on earth it was possible for Miss Thayne, who had never yet travelled further from Thayne Hall than Bath or Bristol, to have become embroiled in the machinations of two unknown criminal lunatics.

The afternoon hours passed with wearying slowness. A minute search of the room revealed no books, no newspapers, nothing with which to beguile the dreary expanse of time. Almost she began to regret her adamant refusal to join her captor for dinner, then she took fresh hold of her perilously weakening resolve and decided she should be planning some means of escape rather than craving the company of a self-avowed villain.

She washed her face vigorously in the now chilly remains of the water Thomas had provided, and made determined efforts to restore her sadly bedraggled hair to some measure of order. She doubted whether the improvement in her appearance was in reality very great, but the cold water seemed to have stimulated her flagging energies, and she felt more capable of coping with the night ahead. The last pin had hardly been placed back in her hair when the door to her room was once more opened.

It was not Thomas but his master who stood framed in the threshold, and Georgiana experienced a fresh thrill of fear as she saw his harsh expression and the uncompromisingly severe lines of his face. He was clad in formal evening clothes of immaculate cut and fit, his linen of evidently high quality, his cravat expertly knotted *à l'Orientale*. It was difficult to quell the resentment that seized her with singular irrationality as she compared her own dishevelled state with her kidnapper's elegant appearance.

"I thought I had made it plain to your servant that I wished to be left alone." Georgiana wondered if her words sounded petulant rather than quelling and dignified as she had intended.

"Thomas conveyed your message to me, that is true." His voice was low and cool, well-modulated and obviously that of a gentleman used to a position of authority. It was suddenly clear to Georgiana that however strange his actions might seem, it was definitely no madman who stood before her. She looked at him angrily.

"In that case, sir, I cannot understand your presence here. Have you not importuned me sufficiently for one day?"

"I regret the necessity for my actions, ma'am. But I, for my part, cannot believe that you would prefer to remain alone here rather than eating with me and perhaps resolving some of the questions which must surely be troubling you."

This remark was so patently true that Georgiana, unable to think of a rational rebuttal, took refuge in anger. "I do not have to explain my actions to you, sir. Please leave me."

She turned away from him in a flurry of temper, storming across to her now-familiar resting place by the window. But this time she was not left alone. The man strode across the room after her, taking her arm with no particular attempt to pretend courtesy. Really angry by now, and more than a little scared, Georgiana twisted herself away, only to find that his grasp was firmer than she had suspected. With a slight exclamation of annoyance he pulled her towards the door.

"Dinner awaits us, madam, and I prefer to eat my food while it is still reasonably warm. Let us not make the ensuing hours more uncomfortable than we need."

Brought to a fresh awareness of her physical vulnerability in comparison to the strength of her captors, Georgiana stumbled ungraciously towards the door. She pursed her lips obstinately, resolved not to speak, even if it was necessary to endure the company of the criminal at her side. Most unwelcome of all was the irritating thought that if only her cousin Freddie looked and spoke as this man did, her recent betrothal would have been considerably easier to tolerate.

CHAPTER
FIVE

THE dining-room retained the faint musty odour that had pervaded the hall, and although the table itself gleamed with polish and was well provided with clean linen, silver and crystal, the remainder of the room appeared distinctly shabby. Thomas was waiting to assist Georgiana to her seat, but there was no sign of any other servant. Georgiana allowed Thomas to pull out her chair, seating herself in sulky silence. Her host – how ludicrous that she had thought of him by such a name! – waited politely until she was quite settled before slipping into a seat immediately opposite her. As soon as Thomas departed, presumably to bring in the dishes of food, the man smiled at her and said, "I think I should introduce myself, Miss Thayne. We can hardly eat a comfortable dinner if you persist in scowling at me in that fashion. Perhaps you will feel our situation is more acceptable if I have a name by which you may mentally castigate me. I am the Marquis of Graydon." He inclined his head in an elegant gesture, worthy of a formal Court reception.

"The Marquis of Graydon!" All Georgiana's noble resolutions about dignified silence fled. She swallowed hastily and managed to stammer, "We had imagined you to be permanently settled abroad, my lord."

"It is true that I have been . . . . away . . . for some time," he acknowledged. "I decided that it was time to return. Your abduction – you see that I don't attempt to disguise my acts under a more acceptable name – is designed to make my return possible."

"But why . . . . how . . ." All Georgiana's suspicions concerning the Marquis' mental stability came flooding back. "My lord, my abduction can have no effect, cannot possibly have any influence upon your decision to return to our neighbourhood. Why, I cannot have been more than a child when your wife . . . when events made you decide to leave!"

"In one sense, Miss Thayne, you are of course entirely right. When I shot my wife – you see that in my absence I have learned to speak frankly – you were indeed a young girl known to me only as the much-loved daughter of a neighbour. It is your relationship to Lady Elizabeth, and your forthcoming marriage to Frederick Thayne, that combine to make you of importance to me." He paused for a few moments. "Your immense fortune, of course, helps to make my . . . scheme . . . virtually foolproof."

Before Georgiana could gather her addled wits to pose a single intelligent question, Thomas had entered and was laying dishes before them. The Marquis of Graydon murmured politely as if conversing with an honoured and intimately-known guest.

"You must forgive us, Miss Thayne, for the necessary simplicity of our meal. Thomas has perforce fulfilled the roles of cook, housekeeper and footman today, so we shall have to content ourselves with a small selection of hot dishes and some fruit and biscuits for dessert." He smiled politely at his servant. "Thank you, Thomas. Miss Thayne and I have a great deal to discuss, so we shall serve ourselves."

Thomas withdrew without comment, and the Marquis of Graydon, with exquisite formality, urged Georgiana to accept a small portion from various of the dishes placed before her. Georgiana spooned food on to her plate quite blindly, with total indifference to the strange combinations that resulted. Blushing furiously, she spoke to the Marquis, her eyes refusing to meet his gaze.

"If, my lord, you are hoping to obtain a large sum for the safe return of my person, I am afraid . . . I am afraid . . ." she swallowed hard and continued, "I am not sure that my relatives would feel that the benefits of my return warranted the expense involved."

To her absolute astonishment, the Marquis burst out laughing.

"What a melancholy reflection, to be sure! Here you are, possessed of one of the larger fortunes in this part of the kingdom, and you're not even sure that your beloved aunt and uncle would bother ransoming you. You should, however, be more cautious in confiding such fears to me. After all, I might decide to cut my losses and murder you forthwith. Surely local gossip has informed you of my dastardly habits for disposing of women who no longer amuse me?"

His last words were tinged with unmistakable bitterness, and with equal bitterness Georgiana responded, "If I am to be murdered, my lord, it seems to me to be a small matter whether it is sooner or later. And even you must surely feel some repugnance at killing a person who was quite unknown to you twenty-four hours ago, simply because her family suffers from a greed that is as great as your own."

There was a small silence and then the Marquis spoke harshly. "I see that this is not a matter for jest. You go too fast in your assumptions. You should remember that you yourself suggested I had abducted you in the hope of financial reward. I made no mention of such a thing and indeed have no need of, or desire for, further funds." He ignored Georgiana's pointed inspection of the room's shabby furnishings and continued to speak.

"For me, Miss Thayne, you are simply a weapon with which I may threaten Lady Elizabeth. And I wish to buy nothing more than her silence, and a measure of social support."

Georgiana looked at the Marquis. "I suppose it would be foolish of me to ask why you wish to threaten my aunt. Only tell me how I can possibly become a weapon in your hands?"

The Marquis allowed his mouth to twist into a small, cynical smile. "You have not thought to ask me how I have spent my afternoon – it has not been passed in idleness, I assure you. The news of your absence is already widely spread throughout the district and although your aunt and uncle were at first greatly alarmed for your safety and spent much time searching the hedgerows for evidence of a mishap, by late this afternoon I am reliably informed that your aunt was beginning to harbour the most unjust suspicions. She now believes that your flight was intentional rather than accidental. She seems to believe you have a strength of character which – I must confess – local rumour has not previously credited to you." Once again the Marquis smiled a little sardonically.

"It appears to have escaped your notice, Miss Thayne, that your reputation is now irretrievably compromised. *We* both know, of course, that no amorous adventure has occurred. But if it is once made public knowledge that you have spent two or three days . . . and nights . . . alone in my company, I think we can allow my unsavoury reputation to create its own version of events. Your . . . ravishment . . . will be known throughout the country within hours of your release."

Georgiana looked straight into his cold grey eyes, and a slow blush started at her neck and suffused her cheeks. "Why?" she whispered. "Why do you have to do this to me?"

The Marquis responded with a touch of irritation that perhaps concealed a feeling of guilt. "I have already explained that I am not compromising *you*, Miss Thayne. I am compromising Lady Elizabeth's niece and Frederick Thayne's betrothed."

"And how is my reputed ravishment expected to assist you in the successful consummation of your plans?" Georgiana's voice was still a mere thread of sound.

"I cannot make you understand my motives, Miss Thayne, without a long and possibly boring excursion into the details of my past. It is clear to me that you know nothing of my previous connection with Lady Elizabeth's family. Perhaps it is better if I merely explain to you what I plan to do, without attempting to justify behaviour that must, I am prepared to admit, seem quite monstrous to you."

"Tell me," said Georgiana dully, "exactly what you plan to do. You must realise that even my fortune will hardly suffice to buy me a respectable husband once today's supposed events are known. Since life offers a female no acceptable alternative to matrimony, I hope that you have weighed the miseries to which you are condemning me against benefits you are expecting – in some mysterious way – to reap."

"There will be no permanent damage to you, Miss Thayne. Indeed, despite my well-known reputation for villainy, it was one of the chief attractions of this scheme for me that in actual fact no real harm accrued to anybody, and several long-festerings wrongs could be quietly righted."

"Tell me," said Georgiana, "precisely how you are planning to achieve this bouquet of miracles?"

The Marquis pushed back his chair from the table and with the satisfied air of a magician about to perform his greatest trick, offered his arm to Georgiana. "Come," he said, "I can see that your appetite is even slighter than my own. Let us sit in more comfortable chairs by the fireside, and I will explain."

He threw two large logs into the hearth, and the dry timber blazed up with a crackle and a faint scent of pine. The Marquis stood with his gleaming boot resting on the fender, looking meditatively into the flames. "I am acquainted with Lady Elizabeth of old," he said. "You do not know, I think, that my wife was Lady Elizabeth's step-sister." He ignored Georgiana's start of astonishment and continued, "You must also forgive me if I seem to talk disparagingly of your betrothed, but he is widely known to be dominated by his mother and it is equally widely known that she intends to keep your pleasantly vast fortune under her family's control. Your uncle's predilection for the gaming tables renders his modest income quite insufficient for the life he, your aunt and your cousin would wish to lead. Rumours of your impending betrothal have been circulating in town for months and I have been waiting, impatiently I confess, to hear confirmation of your engagement to Frederick Thayne. That news reached me last night."

With some amazement, Georgiana registered that the dinner at which her aunt so cunningly betrayed news of her engagement had only occurred the night before, and that her own abduction – which now seemed to have happened in a different century – had only taken place that morning.

"I suppose it is unnecessary for me to ask how news of my engagement travelled so fast," she said. "Doubtless one of my servants is first cousin to one of yours."

The Marquis smiled, lighting his harsh features with a sudden and miraculous touch of gaiety. "You are almost correct. Your housekeeper is aunt to my senior housemaid."

With some asperity Georgiana remarked, "I can only express astonishment that news of your arrival in the district was denied to us. With such a close link between our two households I would have expected communications to be almost instantaneous. I am amazed at that blanket of silence that has been thrown over your highly interesting arrival."

"Well, you see," said the Marquis apologetically, "although this is the first time *we* have had occasion to meet, my presence in the district is not so great a matter of astonishment to my servants, who are quite accustomed to having me visit the estate. It was only when Jenny, my housemaid, learned that *this* time I was planning a permanent return to Graydon Place that she thought the news important enough to carry to her aunt. It so happened that her first opportunity to walk over to Thayne Hall arrived yesterday evening and your housekeeper was delighted to be able to pass on the interesting news of your engagement."

"Ah yes," said Georgiana, "my engagement. You still have not explained to me how my marriage is of any possible interest to you and your plans involving Aunt Elizabeth."

The Marquis turned slightly so that he spoke to the

fire rather than to Georgiana. "Your aunt will never give up your fortune if *any* other course is open to her. I therefore propose to return to Thayne Hall with you and threaten your aunt with a scandal of major proportions. Or, if she is prepared to co-operate with me, I will undertake never to reveal that we have been alone together. Lady Elizabeth has only to agree that she will accept my permanent return to Graydon Place and that she will exert her influence to ensure that neither Lord Thayne nor Frederick blackballs my request for readmittance to the London clubs from which I resigned when my wife died. At that time, your aunt achieved my social ostracism almost single-handedly. Now I wish her to be responsible for my readmission to the life which was mine from birth."

The Marquis turned and glanced sardonically at Georgiana. "When we are young, Miss Thayne, we think that our neighbours are very dull sort of people. At thirty-five, I have discovered that I no longer wish to be an exile, and only your aunt can gain me readmission into the local fold."

Georgiana stared at the Marquis, her expression of blank incomprehension for once entirely unfeigned. "But why should my aunt fear rumours concerning my reputation, however outrageous they may be? If, as you insist, she cares nothing for me and wants only to secure my fortune for Freddie, why should she care about an abduction that she knows has resulted in no real harm to my person? Even the most scandalous *on dits* must surely eventually lose their savour, and interest in my pre-marital affairs will simply die away once I am wed to Freddie."

"You are naïve, Miss Thayne," said the Marquis. "I can offer a personal testimonial to the length of public memory for a really savoury scandal." Swiftly he drew in his breath and walked angrily over to the table, pouring wine into his glass with reckless disregard for the stains spreading over the white lace tablecloth.

"In fact, Miss Thayne, your aunt will be unable to ignore my threats. Lady Elizabeth is blessed with a highly obliging son. But Freddie has been grossly over-indulged and can, as a consequence, become disast-rously obstinate. I fear that Freddie would not be able to tolerate the thought of being married to . . . forgive me . . . a second-hand bride. Like all weak persons," the Marquis added conversationally, "Freddie has an inflated regard for the vagaries of public opinion. Your aunt knows that Freddie will never marry you once the tatters of so distasteful a scandal hang around you, no matter what threats or inducements she attempts to offer. We both know that Freddie's enthusiasm for the marriage is of the most modest order – indeed his reluctance to come to the point despite his unhappy financial position has been one of the talking-points of town – and I'm afraid your public loss of virtue would be the final straw that pushed him out of sullen resis-tance and into outright rebellion."

With heightened colour, Georgiana rose from her seat. "It is not enough that you must bring me here in this despicable fashion and force me to listen to the insults you have been heaping upon my family. Now you must submit me to the further humiliation of hear-ing that all London knows that my betrothed can hardly tolerate the thought of marriage to me. I bid you good-night, my lord, and I trust that in the morning rational-ity – and a measure of Christian charity – will have returned to guide your actions."

Without bothering to look again at the Marquis,

Georgiana walked swiftly to the heavy doors barring the exit from the dining-room. To her chagrin she found the handles were too old and stiff to yield, and she was unable to swing open the doors as quickly as she wished. Before she could escape into the hallway, the Marquis was behind her, grabbing her around the waist and propelling her back towards the centre of the room. Angered and frustrated to a point beyond caution, Georgiana twisted in his arms, struggling to free herself from his clasp which had suddenly tightened. With a sudden expression of extreme curiosity, the Marquis held her some distance away from his body, while still retaining a firm grip on her arms.

"Why, Miss Thayne, what's this? All night I have been intrigued by the startling contrast between that entrancing slender neck, those delicate wrists and your . . . robust . . . waistline. Now it seems that there is a mystery here indeed, for unless I am mistaken – which I doubt – your waist has been padded by a considerable volume of cloth." The Marquis peered at her intently. "And your cheeks – that unnatural bulge that totally destroys the line of your profile. I believe that is false also! Is it possible that you have actually padded your cheeks? What conceivable cause can you have for such actions?"

White-cheeked, Georgiana turned to face him. "Fortunately, my lord, no explanation is necessary. Your scheme succeeds or fails without co-operation from me. Now I am tired and in some discomfort after the manner in which you . . . held . . . me. May I please have your permission to retire?"

The Marquis allowed his hands to fall against his sides, and with a gesture eloquent of his disinterest in Georgiana's petty deceptions he strode over to the decanter of port. As he poured a generous measure into a fresh glass he spoke with cool indifference.

"As you please, Miss Thayne. I would simply remind you that the duration of your stay under my roof depends entirely upon my goodwill. The sooner you are prepared to discuss the issues between us sensibly, the sooner you will be returned to the anxiously awaiting arms of your family."

Georgiana tossed her head in a gesture that would have drawn amazed glances from the household at Thayne Hall used to the meek and feeble-witted Miss Thayne, but she did not deign to reply. She was arrested in her impassioned and (she hoped) dignified sweep from the room by a soft laugh. She paused but did not turn around and the patronising tones of the Marquis fell upon her outraged ears.

"It seems a mundane note upon which to end a scene of such high drama, Miss Thayne, but you will be relieved to know that Thomas has in possession brushes, toothpowder, combs and several other necessary items of a similar nature. I am sure you will be relieved to know that you can retire tonight well-groomed, even if imprisoned. Goodnight, Miss Thayne."

CHAPTER
SIX

GEORGIANA was not sure when the idea of revenge first took firm hold in her mind. She retired to bed with her thoughts seemingly in a tumbling mass of confusion and panic, and woke up in the morning possessed of an unnatural icy calmness that might, in more normal circumstances, have given her pause to consider the widom of decisions made in the thrall of such a mood. She accepted morning chocolate from Thomas, which he left outside her bedchamber door after knocking to ensure that she was awake, and responded politely to his intimation that breakfast would be ready within the hour. She accepted a jug of hot water delivered outside her door in a similar manner, and after washing sat down before the dressing table to examine her appearance with a disapassionate scrutiny that had never recently seemed possible.

In view of the rapid changes that had occurred in her life over the past few days it seemed suddenly utterly childish to continue with a disguise that no longer served any useful purpose. She therefore refrained from padding her cheeks with small squares of cotton and discarded the soft length of white cambric which was normally bound in enveloping folds around her naturally trim waistline. It was almost a relief to comb out the frizzled remnants of her former curls and to sweep her hair up in the smooth, simple style that was to her genuine taste. Of course her gown, crumpled and slightly soiled after two days of wear, was not improved in appearance, since it now hung in limp and voluminous folds about her suddenly emaciated person. However – she shrugged her shoulders in silent resignation – despite the bedraggled gown her appearance presented a startling contrast with the bundled and frilly gaucheness that Miss Thayne was accustomed to showing to the world.

There was no denying the pleasure to be derived from her remarkably transformed looks, and Georgiana stared unwinkingly at the flattering reflection in the looking-glass. *Ha!* thought Georgiana in silent triumph, *now I shall show him!*

On this satisfactory note she marched over to her bedroom door, quite prepared to do battle with whoever might be waiting on the other side, and quite unprepared to examine the precise direction in which her somewhat cryptic thoughts were leading her.

She was less surprised than she might have been to find the door unlocked, because it had occurred to her during the night that a great many of the harsher aspects of her abduction had been designed to intimidate rather than actually to imprison. It was quite clear that without a horse, and isolated in the midst of a wide stretch of overgrown countryside, the Marquis of Graydon could not realistically anticipate her immediate escape, particularly since Georgiana had no idea of which direction to flee in search of succour.

Thomas was waiting in the hall as she descended the shabby staircase, ostensibly to direct her footsteps towards the dining-parlour, but more probably, Georgiana thought wryly, to prevent her taking a sudden flight through the front door. She accepted his directions with a courteous nod of the head, and opened the heavy doors that had foiled her so disastrously the night before. She could not altogether repress a slight shiver of nervous excitement as she saw the effect of her altered appearance upon the Marquis. He half rose to his feet, the habitual hauteur of his expression quite obliterated by a flush of astonishment.

He spoke with a sudden, unexpected charm. "There is no need to ask if your night's sleep has refreshed you." He paused a moment and then smiled. "And perhaps I should not be so indelicate as to mention to you how greatly imprisonment has improved your figure!"

Georgiana stiffened, more than ready to retaliate in kind, then remembered her half-formed plans and managed to stretch her lips into a somewhat forced smile. She sank gracefully into the chair the Marquis was holding for her and accepted some of the soft white bread and sweet preserves he offered to her. Before the Marquis could speak, Georgiana rushed into the slight silence.

"The night has indeed brought counsel, my lord. *I* do not wish to be a captive and *you* must be anxious to resume your more normal pattern of living." Unable to restrain herself, she remarked acidly, "I cannot think that my bedchamber is used to such solitary and dowdily respectable occupants if the incredibly vulgar bed hangings . . ." She glimpsed the Marquis' expression and hastily brought her speech to a halt. "Yes, well, I intended to suggest to you that your purpose has surely now been achieved and there is no need for us to continue in this fashion any longer. If you will agree to return me to my family today, it will relieve the anxieties of those who wait for news of me. I cannot see that there is any way in which you could expect me to thwart the plans you have in regard to my aunt, whether I return now or a day later."

The Marquis was silent for a few moments as he considered Georgiana's words. The hesitancy of his final response took Georgiana somewhat by surprise, for she had judged him to be a man of quick and firm decisions.

"I confess that I can see no real reason to delay your return. No doubt there are people in the village who are concerned for your safety, and others are wasting valuable farming time in searching for you. However, Miss Thayne, I do not trust you, and I would dearly love to read the thoughts that are undoubtedly running through the agile brain concealed behind your simpering expression. Remember, I have already caught you out in one unexplained deception, and I have no wish to find myself in the middle of another of your childish plots. *You* would undoubtedly merely be playing. *I* have reached a point in my life when I know it is time to face up to the scandals of the past and start afresh."

"Indeed, my lord, you have decided wisely! Surely there can be no better way to squash remembrance of past misdeeds than to reintroduce yourself into the neighbourhood by way of a fresh scandal?"

Immediately Georgiana had spoken she could have bitten off her tongue. She felt a frustrating sense of shared humour with this man that caused her to speak to him so unguardedly, when for years she had remained aloof and untouched in the face of endless provocation from her uncle, her aunt and especially from her cousin Freddie.

The Marquis looked at her coldly. "Your conversation, Miss Thayne, does not leave me wishing for a prolongation of our enforced *ménage-à-deux*. I have my travelling chaise here, and I shall ask Thomas to harness the necessary horses. If you wish to ready yourself for the journey back to Thayne Hall, I imagine Thomas will have the chaise outside the front door in half an hour." He rose to his feet.

"Forgive me if I don't escort you to your room. The remembered temptations of those vulgar bed hangings might prove too much for my self-control."

White-lipped, Georgiana rose to her feet. "You lose no opportunity to insult me, my lord, but since I look forward to the moment of my release, I shall rejoin you within the half-hour."

The spring weather had once again proven its unreliability and it was distinctly chilly as the Marquis handed Georgiana up into the carriage. He looked at her thin dress with some concern and then spoke abruptly. "I had forgotten that you have no warmer garments with you." He bent down and spoke quiet instructions to Thomas and the servant returned shortly carrying an elegant velvet evening cloak. Not looking at Georgiana, the Marquis spoke in clipped accents. "I beg you will place this cloak about your shoulders. I recognize that it is not a suitable piece of clothing for this time of day, but I have nothing else to offer you."

Georgiana, torn between amused annoyance at wearing what was probably a discarded garment from the wardrobe of a lady of highly doubtful virtue, and relief that she was not expected to freeze, wrapped the cloak tightly around her body and murmured some brief words of thanks. She was so busy pulling her incoherent thoughts and nebulous plans into some form of order, that she paid no attention to the passing scenery nor to the lengthening silence between the Marquis and herself. She was returned to a proper sense of her exact surroundings by the sound of the Marquis's voice.

"I see that I am to be reprimanded, Miss Thayne. But do you not think our journey could be more easily beguiled if we engaged in a little light conversation?"

Since Georgiana could hardly reply that she had been preoccupied in plotting his downfall rather than administering a rebuke for past misdeeds, it was not easy to find a response. Finally she spoke. "My social training has been limited in scope, my lord, and has not equipped me to make frivolous conversation with kidnappers. Do you suggest we admire the scenery, or perhaps we should search our memories for acquaintances we may have in common?"

The Marquis looked at her with some amusement. "I cam sure we need not be reduced to such straits," he said. "The curiosity of your sex is well known. Surely you could find some personal questions with which to plague me? Have you really so little interest in the past connections between my family and your own?"

A new note of exasperation had entered his voice and Georgiana wondered for a fleeting moment if he was finding this abduction more of a burden on his conscience than he had anticipated. Anxious to test him, she spoke sweetly. "Why, if you would care to attempt some justification of your actions, my lord, I should be quite happy to listen. I must warn you, however, that I find it astonishingly difficult to understand why I – who have certainly played no part in any past wrongs that may have been done you – should be made the chief victim in your schemes."

The Marquis replied angrily, "Since you have been destined for several years to marry your cousin, and since I am merely ensuring that the anticipated marriage will occur, I do not accept that you are a victim, Miss Thayne. You have suffered no harm, no discomfort . . .''

"How can you say that?" Georgiana cried. "Indeed, I may have few physical injuries, although I now bear several bruises that were certainly not present two days ago. But what of my mental state? Have you no feelings at all? Can you not begin to understand the wild and terrifying fancies that filled my mind when you and your servant seized me, and then left me incarcerated for hours on my own – and in *such* a room!"

Her cheeks whitened at the memory, for suddenly the events of the past day and night seemed more terrifying in retrospect than they had even in actuality. Her hand trembled slightly and she thrust it beneath her cloak in an attempt to regain control of her vanishing calmness of manner.

She felt the Marquis place his hand gently on her arm, and even through the velvet cloak she could feel the warm strength that seemed to reach out and reassure her. Furious with herself for allowing the Marquis to creep under her guard, she jerked her arm hastily away, and was rewarded with an instant reprimand. "The horses, Miss Thayne! Have you no sense?"

But once the horses were again under perfect control, Georgiana acknowledged to herself that information could only be helpful in co-ordinating the thin threads of her planning, so she turned to the Marquis and spoke calmly.

"I'm sorry, my lord, let us try once again to be civil to one another. There are indeed questions I would like to ask that I feel sure you would be prepared to answer. Firstly, where did I . . . we . . . spend the night? and secondly, where have you been these past few years? For it occurs to me that you have probably not been abroad since you seem so well informed upon local matters."

The Marquis was silent for a while and then spoke thoughtfully. "We were at the Dower House on my estate. As you know, my land (which includes the woods in which I found you wandering, by the way) marches along the northern boundary of your property. The Dower House is at the extreme northern end of my land. As you know, I have not used Graydon Place in recent years, but it has sometimes suited me to have a rural retreat available, and that is why I chose to have the Dower House partially refurbished."

Georgiana was not altogether successful in concealing an indignant toss of the head as she visualised the sort of purpose for which the Marquis normally required his rural retreat.

"I can see that those bed hangings were definitely a mistake," the Marquis murmured, and then fell hastily silent as he caught Georgiana's irate gaze. "You will have realised," he continued after a suitable pause, "that yesterday we rode across country and accomplished the journey in some forty minutes. By road we must take a considerably longer route, and I anticipate that we shall not be back at Thayne Hall for another half-hour at least."

"And my second question, my lord?" Georgiana prompted when the Marquis fell silent.

"As you suspected," he said, "I have not been out of England except briefly. At the time the scandal broke over my largely unsuspecting head, I gave out the news that I was leaving for Italy. In fact, my wife had rendered me as close to penniless as made no odds, and

I had no particular desire to join the band of impoverished British exiles who haunt the Italian cities. I therefore went to London and disappeared very successfully."

"I would not have thought London a particularly easy place in which to hide from a scandal," remarked Georgiana." After all, even I know that there one is for ever encountering old acquaintances, even if you did take the elementary precaution of resigning from all your clubs."

The Marquis laughed scornfully, torn between bitterness and amusement. "Even you, Miss Thayne, are a victim of your prejudices. You see London as a very small town, with narrowly defined limits. I did not live in the London *you* know at all. I exiled myself to the City, and used the resources of my property here to buy into some of the merchant ventures undertaken by the city tradesmen. I lived for almost six years in Cheapside with the man who eventually allowed me to become his partner. I could not have been more effectively isolated from contact with my former acquaintances if I had emigrated to the shores of America."

"I see." Georgiana could scarcely cope with the bewildering mass of new information. It seemed that every conversation they had necessitated a change in her impression of the Marquis' character and personality. "But still, my lord, you remained remarkably well informed of the doings of the *haut ton*, and the affairs of my family in particular."

"We have already discussed the prodigious skills of servants in eliciting information that their masters believe to be entirely private. Thomas undoubtedly knows more about me, and about London society in general, than I know myself."

"You are lucky to enjoy the services of so loyal a retainer," Georgiana retorted with some asperity.

"Indeed." The Marquis paid no attention to her attempt at sarcasm. "We have been companions in crime from an early age. His father was once butler at Graydon Place and Thomas, I believe, managed to create almost as much mayhem below stairs as I was creating in my mother's drawing rooms. Both our respective parents confidently prophesied that we would come to disastrous and disgraceful ends."

Georgiana was unable to resist laughing. "It seems we must agree that both your father and his butler were excellent prophets. You may not yet have reached the end of the road, but your paths seem fairly clearly mapped out – and I am sure they lead disastrously downwards!"

The Marquis looked at her in silence, and then remarked with supreme irrelevance, "You should laugh more often. It is highly becoming."

Georgiana blushed and spoke hurriedly. "We seem to be approaching Thayne Hall, since I begin to recognise the countryside. You have not yet attempted to explain to me the connection between Lady Elizabeth and your late . . . wife."

"Oh, that!" the Marquis responded airily. "Why, there is no mystery at all. Lady Elizabeth will not permit my name to be mentioned in her presence, which is why you remained unaware of the relationship her step-sister had to me. Your father died very shortly after my wife, and since you were still in the schoolroom at the time, it is no wonder that the full story of my misdeeds has remained unknown to you. There is, after all, no one to enlighten you."

Georgiana said nothing, although she made a silent

vow to seek out Miss Harris and demand an immediate explanation of that lady's unjustifiable reticence on a topic likely to be of such burning interest to her former pupil. The amusing tales of the Wicked Marquis, Georgiana now realised, were nothing more than inventions of her governess' fertile imagination, designed probably to keep Georgiana from prying too deeply into a scandal that touched her own family circle. Miss Harris was a dear lady and a splendid teacher, but the circumstances of her life had forced the governess into accepting and even encouraging fairly rigid standards of propriety where her charges were concerned. Seeing that Georgiana was not prepared to comment, the Marquis continued in the same lightly mocking voice.

"You have to understand that Lady Chloë, my Marchioness, was a vision of classical loveliness, and she was worshipped by her entire family – especially by her elder step-sister, your Aunt Elizabeth. How privileged I knew myself to be when I was allowed to marry her! One of the most startling beauties of the decade, and from the very *best* of families naturally. So deep were my own feelings that I never paused to question whether Lady Chloë desired the match as much as I did myself."

The Marquis turned away swiftly, but not quite in time to conceal the bitter twist of his lips. He seemed lost in painful memories for a few moments and Georgiana, conscious of the increasing proximity of Thayne Hall, asked, "What happened after your marriage, my lord?"

The Marquis was again in control of his emotions. "Oh," he said carelessly, "hardly were we safely married when, profligate wretch that I am, I squandered her modest dowry and retreated to a life of debauchery in

London. I was finally persuaded to return to Graydon
Hall, and there compounded by villainy by murdering
my neglected bride. She, you must understand, had
done nothing more wicked during the three years of our
marriage than seek innocent solace with my cousin . . .
and several dozen other gentlemen anxious to succour
such a sorrowing and injured bride.

"You cannot, of course, be at all surprised," the
Marquis continued, "that in these horrible circumstances your aunt made every effort to advertise the
nature of my crimes over the widest possible area, and
with supreme moral righteousness ensured that the
doors of Society were closed rather abruptly in my face.
It was only the fact that Thomas swore I had aimed my
pistol in self-defence – and not even in the direction of
Lady Chloë – that prevented your aunt from persuad-
ing the local justices to have me arrested on a charge of
murder."

Laughingly he examined Georgiana's horror-struck
expression, quite misinterpreting the impenetrable silence that had seized her.

"Surely now, Miss Thayne, you can understand that
a mere abduction is nothing to me or to my servant.
Your recent . . . discomforts . . . can be dismissed as
mere bagatelles to a man guilty of so prolific and hein-
ous a list of crimes."

Georgiana looked directly into the hard grey eyes
above her. "You are vastly mistaken in my character,
my lord, if you imagine that I am prepared to take such
a story at face value. I have lived with Lady Elizabeth
for seven years, and I have known our neighbours all of
my adult life. I am perfectly well able to understand
that there may be quite other interpretations of the facts
you have recounted – interpretations that would be

less acceptable to my aunt and the neighbours, perhaps, but nevertheless closer to the truth. If you planned to terrorize me with this tale of past wickedness, my lord, I regret that I must tell you you have wasted your time."

The Marquis spoke with some exasperation. "I begin to wonder if I have not been wasting my time since the moment I first took you up on poor Diabolo – although the memory of that incident perhaps recompenses me for much of what has followed!"

"Even you, my lord, should appreciate that it is ungentlemanlike to refer to the indelicate manner in which it was necessary to handle my person when forcing me into Diabolo's saddle. I think, my lord . . ."

"Enough!" the Marquis protested. "It is bad enough to listen to your constant scolds without being subjected to yet another sentence beginning, 'I think, my lord'." His eyes laughed silently at her discomposure. "Surely the informality of our acquaintance this far ought to induce you to address me as Lord Graydon at the very least? I accept that it would be overly optimistic to indulge the hope that you might call me Julian, which is my given name, but I do not despair of plain Graydon before this affair is entirely over."

"Why no, my lord," said Georgiana sweetly. "Before this affair is entirely over I am quite sure I might be persuaded to address you with greater informality."

"Now what the devil do you mean by that remark?" asked the Marquis with sudden suspicion.

"Why nothing, Lord Graydon. And may I point out that we are approaching my home? I see we have quite a reception committee waiting to greet us."

She opened her eyes very wide so that the Marquis for the first time received the full benefit of their unusual intensity of colour. He drew in a sudden, sharp breath but there was no time to speak for Johnson, the butler, was running out of the house in a manner quite unlike his normal dignified gait, and three or four footmen stood round waiting anxiously to to assist Georgiana in her descent from the chaise.

"Oh Miss Thayne, it's wonderful to see you back safely," said Johnson. "We didn't know what to think when we couldn't find you yesterday morning. I thought you'd been killed, I did that, although Mrs. Bridges said it was more likely . . ."

Horrified at the course of his own rambling speech, the butler fell hastily silent, his face reverting to its normal mask of lugubrious imperturbability. Puffing out his chest he offered a solicitous arm to Miss Thayne, calling out peremptory orders to the footmen and to the grooms who had by now appeared from the back of the house. "We were agreed you'd been set upon by gypsies, ma'am. I'm right pleased to see you safe home again."

CHAPTER
SEVEN

THE Marquis of Graydon watched Georgiana's return into the bosom of her family home with a face entirely devoid of any visible emotion. An aura of slightly bored cynicism hung over his entire person, and the butler could hardly wait to return and discover the name of Miss Thayne's rescuer. As soon as Georgiana had been safely deposited on the inside of the massive oak door-way, Johnson could feel his normal composure return and he looked with intense but well-concealed interest at the tall, magnificently attired gentleman stepping down from the chaise that had brought Miss Thayne back to the Hall. It really seemed as though Mrs. Bridges might be right in maintaining that Georgiana had run away from a forced marriage with her cousin Frederick, although how simple-minded Miss Thayne had ever managed to find so sophisticated a protector Johnson could not begin to imagine. Much to the butler's annoyance, the housekeeper often did seem to have more idea of what was going on in the house than he did, despite the advantage of his position and his constant involvement in the goings and comings of the Family.

Johnson examined the immaculate tailoring of the gentleman's riding-coat and thought silently that nobody could blame poor Miss Thayne for preferring this bang-up Town swell to her unfortunate cousin.

Well aware that a splendid family drama was about to be enacted, Johnson watched the footmen escort the visitor up the porticoed steps into the reception area. The mask of the perfect servant was firmly in place as he coughed politely before speaking.

"I expect you will wish to speak to the head of the family, sir. May I ask what name I should give to Lord Thayne if he is at home?"

The gentleman looked at Johnson thoughtfully for several moments then he said, "I am the Marquis of Graydon. I wish to speak to Lady Elizabeth Thayne rather than to Baron Thayne. If Lady Elizabeth is not at home I am prepared to wait for her return."

"Very good, my lord." The butler could hardly contain his excitement. The drama was becoming greater by the moment. "I will see if Lady Elizabeth is able to receive visitors. I know that she has been waiting with great . . . agitation . . . for Miss Thayne's return."

At these words, the butler suddenly remembered Miss Thayne's presence and turned round to find that she was sitting quietly on a chair in a dark corner. Johnson felt rather guilty at having forgotten her return in the excitement of escorting the notorious Marquis of Graydon into Thayne Hall, but he excused himself mentally on the grounds that she was always such a quiet, unassuming dab of a thing that it was no wonder she so often got neglected. The Marquis of Graydon was speaking to her now, and the butler strained unashamedly to hear what was being discussed.

"I am sure you will wish to retire to your rooms after such an ordeal," the Marquis said. He did not want to examine the confusion of feelings that were threatening to break in upon his carefully laid plans. He only knew it was necessary to remove Georgiana from the scene as swiftly as possible. "I imagine that we shall not be permitted to speak after my interview with your aunt," he added lightly, "so I must bid you *au revoir*. You see that I do not say goodbye, for I am sure that we shall see one another in town once you are safely married and I am safely returned to the warm embrace of London society."

The flippant words were hard to utter, so that his voice sounded brusque and his bow held a subtle mockery as he bent over Georgiana's hand.

She could not know that the mockery was directed towards himself, and her previous anger crystallised into firm resolve. Raising her voice so that Johnson could hear her words quite plainly she said, "But I am not planning to leave you now. We shall see my aunt together."

Before the Marquis could protest, Georgiana turned to the butler. "Johnson, please bring my aunt to the yellow salon as quickly as possible. I am not tired, and so the Marquis of Graydon and I can await my aunt's arrival together."

"Yes, Miss Thayne." Johnson paused for a few discreet moments to see if the Marquis would have the effrontery to disagree with these instructions. He finally moved regretfully towards Lady Elizabeth's private suite of rooms, accepting that even the notorious Marquis of Graydon was not about to commit the dreadful social solecism of countermanding Miss Thayne's orders in her own home, however much he might have wished to do so.

The Marquis waited until Johnson's back had disappeared round the corner and then grabbed Georgiana's wrist, pulling her unceremoniously in the nearest salon and slamming the door shut behind him.

"Just what is this idea of remaining present while I am talking with your aunt? Does it appeal to some warped, feminine instinct in you to observe the embarrassment and discomfiture of others? I can assure you that nothing about this forthcoming scene is likely to be pleasant. Would it not be preferable to retire to the comfort of your room while you have the chance?"

Georgiana spoke very softly. "I take no particular pleasure in observing other people's anger, my lord. But it is *my* future which is being tossed about like a gambling counter between you and my aunt. I think I am at least entitled to hear the manner in which I am married off."

"I beg leave to disagree with you ma'am. I must ask you to return to your chamber." The Marquis took Georgiana's arm once again, no doubt with the intention of removing her forcibly since arguments seemed to be having so little effect. He failed to hear the click of the door-handle turning, and was therefore paralysed with astonishment when he suddenly felt Georgiana's body collapse against his waistcoat, her head resting comfortably against the revers of his coat as she murmured achingly, "Oh, Julian, what are we to do?"

"Ma'am . . . er . . . Miss Thayne . . . er . . . Georgiana . . .?"

For once the Marquis seemed utterly bereft of speech until he observed the malicious gleam in the pair of exceptionally bright blue eyes staring up at him from the protection of his waistcoat. Instantly he thrust Georgiana away from him, whirling round to meet the icy stare of Lady Elizabeth, looking every inch the fourth Baroness Thayne. To crown his exasperation, Johnson's figure remained framed in the doorway, interest and astonishment scarcely concealed behind a professionally blank expression.

Without removing her eyes from the Marquis, Lady Elizabeth spoke. "You may leave us, Johnson." She turned slightly. "I trust you have some satisfactory explanation for your prolonged absence, Georgiana?"

Georgiana hung her head and remained strangely silent. It seemed to the Marquis that almost in front of his bewildered gaze her entire personality changed as a look of frightened and bovine stupidity settled over her features. The Marquis spoke impatiently, anxious to remove himself from a situation that he now realised was not fully under his control.

"Miss Thayne, please sit down. I am sure you have your aunt's permission. Lady Elizabeth, may I assist you to a seat on the sofa?"

"I am perfectly capable of seating myself to my satisfaction in my own home, my lord, but I prefer to stand. Do you have something you wish to say to me before I ask you to leave? You realise, I am sure, that in normal circumstances you would never have been allowed to cross the threshold of any house belonging to me."

The Marquis bowed ironically. "Indeed, Lady Elizabeth, your feelings on this subject are only too well known to me. I will endeavour to spare you the discomfort of too large a dose of my presence by coming straight to the point. Your niece, Miss Thayne, has been missing for an entire day and a night. The local farmers and labourers have all been out scouring the countryside for her, so her absence from home is a matter of public knowledge. You will probably be interested to learn, Lady Elizabeth, that your niece spent yesterday and last night alone with me in the Dower House that stands on my property."

Lady Elizabeth started to speak, but was politely silenced by the Marquis. "Pray allow me to finish, madam, since I am sure you will wish to know the whole story before you make any rash comments. For various reasons that are well known to you, I have not publicly returned to Graydon Place for six years. However, you may have heard – the country is a marvellous place for gossip, is it not? – that the Dower House was partially renovated some three years ago when I first began to make brief, private visits to my estates. Since the time of its renovation it has been used exclusively as . . . how shall I describe it?"

The Marquis paused delicately and examined his quizzing glass with spurious concentration. "One does not wish to sully female ears with sordid details," he said finally. "You, Lady Elizabeth, who know me so well, will understand I am sure that I sometimes felt the need for a *special* retreat to accommodate some of the ladies of my acquaintance. The excellent parties I have given at the Dower House have become somewhat notorious among the servants of the district, I believe."

Lady Elizabeth turned to the huddled figure of her niece. "How could you!" she exclaimed. "How could you possibly *consort* with such a man?"

Georgiana made no reply – it was hard to think of an appropriate one on the spur of the moment – and the Marquis eventually came to her rescue. "Before you berate Miss Thayne too severely," he intervened, "I should tell you that she accompanied me most reluctantly, and I am happy to assure you that no . . . er . . . harm of any sort befell her. But we both know that her cousin – who has such a bourgeois sense of respectability, don't you feel? – might not care to marry a girl who has spent so much time alone with such an infamous rake . . . It would be disastrous to your plans, I think, if poor Frederick should ever get to hear of this escapade."

Pale with anger, Lady Elizabeth sank on to the sofa in a rustle of puce satin. "I am quite sure that you have a solution to this dilemma" she remarked, "and I suppose you have already concocted some outrageous lie to explain how *you* came to return my niece to her family. Georgiana may tell me later exactly how she came to place herself in your power, although I have long since wondered whether she can be considered responsible for her own actions. However, you may as well tell me exactly what price you anticipate extorting for your silence? I have no doubt that you are in need of money again, just as you always were, but you are mistaken if you believe that I have a fortune ready and waiting to pour into your lap."

The Marquis looked at her disdainfully. "You always did have an appalling mercenary mind, my dear sister-in-law." Lady Elizabeth winced and he continued blandly, "The payment I am expecting from you is very small. I merely wish you to accept my return to the neighbourhood, to let your friends and acquaintances know that I may be present at balls and soirées and parties to which you and Lord Thayne are invited. Oh yes! And I need you to ensure that neither Cousin Frederick nor Lord Thayne blackballs my admission to White's or any of the other London clubs that I may decide to join once again."

Lady Elizabeth looked at the Marquis, her well-bred face distorted by the depths of her disgust. "You call that a small payment, my lord Marquis?" She drew a shuddering breath. "Just to see you is to be reminded of my dearest Chloë, and the agonies to which you subjected her with your appalling and debauched behaviour. I could not endure my life if I never knew when you might be present at the same gathering as myself."

"No?" The Marquis looked at her coldly, then spoke through tight lips. "Your feelings for your sister, madam, do credit to your heart but no credit at all to your commonsense or to your sensitivity. However . . ."

Abruptly he pulled himself to full height and turned back to his contemplation of the fireplace. "You must decide whether you prefer to have Miss Thayne's money for Frederick, or my continued absence 'abroad'." He laughed briefly as he saw Lady Elizabeth's pained expression. "Forgive the crudity of my expression, madam. The choice between money or no money remains the same however delicately you may care to express it."

Lady Elizabeth's reply was lost in a brief knock at the door was swiftly followed by the entry of Viscount Benham. He spoke immediately to Lady Elizabeth.

"Forgive me, my dear, for intruding upon you in these clothes. I was riding round the estate in the vague hope of hearing word of my god-daughter when one of your grooms rode up with the happy news that Georgiana had been safely restored to us. I understand from the butler that she is in here with you?"

At his words, Lady Elizabeth and the Marquis of Graydon both turned to the chair where Georgiana had seated herself, both feeling slightly irritated that in the heat of their conversation they had allowed her presence to remain undisturbed. Both found themselves incapable of immediate speech when a sobbing Georgiana flung herself in a dramatic appeal at the Viscount's feet.

"Oh sir, I am betrayed! I have been so wicked and now I am to be punished! Please, I beg of you, help me!"

During the twenty-four hours of Georgiana's disappearance, Viscount Benham's understanding of the female species had increased not one iota. His guilty conscience, however, had begun to burden him considerably. Since he was an honourable, if overworked, gentleman, he had passed the night wondering uneasily if his godchild might not have done something desperate rather than marry her cousin Freddie. He had known all along, of course, that she was unenthusiastic about the match, but it was only her disappearance that caused him to think that Georgiana's wishes should be given some weight in any decision that was reached concerning her future. He therefore looked at the huddled white mass at his feet with a mixture of embarrassment and sympathy. His own experiences with women prevented him from seeing anything extraordinary in the extravagant emotionalism of Georgiana's appeal. He patted his godchild's head awkwardly in a somewhat confused gesture of comfort and goodwill, meanwhile managing to ask in a tolerably composed manner for some explanation of Georgiana's distress.

The Marquis and Lady Elizabeth both started to speak at once. Above their accusing tones, Georgiana's voice was heard, soft but amazingly clear and penetrating. "Sir, I must calm myself and tell you the whole story. I beg you to forgive me for my foolishness and to help me before I am abandoned by the man who once pledged to support me for ever!"

It seemed that she was about to be overcome by tears, but with a struggle she regained control of her quivering voice and sank back on to her satin chair.

Viscount Benham patted her hand, and hoped very much that there would not be too much in his god-child's story that he would have to forgive. Lady Elizabeth was staring at her niece in silent amazement, for once utterly incapable of speech as she started to take full measure of all the changes in he niece's appear-ance and manner. The Marquis of Graydon also remained silent, but he seemed lost in calculations of his own and Georgiana resolutely avoided looking at him as she started her story.

"You must know, sir, that I have often been very lonely here since my parents died, and for several years I have been in the habit of walking through the grounds alone to seek refreshment and solace in the beauties of nature." She paused while the Viscount nodded approvingly. It was well known that the female brain, being incapable of coping with weighty problems, often needed frivolous diversions not required by the sturdier constitutions of English gentlemen.

"At first, when I was younger," Georgiana con-tinued, "I was always accompanied by my governess, but for the past two years it has been agreed that I am at liberty to go unattended provided I do not leave the grounds of Thayne Hall. About a year ago, when I was walking through the dear little woods on our northern boundary, I encountered a gentleman." Georgiana paused dramatically, then allowed her head to hang low as she whispered, "It was the Marquis of Graydon."

Lady Elizabeth finally spoke. "What were you think-ing of?" she asked Georgiana. "How could you speak to such a man, knowing what my feelings must be? Not to mention the outrageous impropriety of such conversa-tions without a proper introduction."

Georgiana managed a convincing blush which was

not difficult since she was forced to hold her breath in an effort not to giggle. Only her aunt could worry about proper introductions at such a moment. She turned again to the Viscount whose expression, she was relieved to see, remained basically sympathetic. "The Marquis told me that he could not meet me honourably in my home," whispered Georgiana, "because he would not be accepted by my aunt. He told me there were . . . incidents . . . in his past that had been misinterpreted by my family." She was improvising wildly, hoping in part to spare her aunt unnecessary pain. "But Julian swore that he loved me and that we should be married one day, as soon as his fortune enabled him to support a wife."

Georgiana turned appealing eyes to her godfather. "I told him of my huge fortune and begged him to agree to marry me at once. But he would not hear of it and said he would never marry me until he could do so without people accusing him of being a fortune-hunter. So you see," she concluded with naive triumph, "I was convinced that he was a man of honour." Pathetically her voice dropped even lower. "How could I know that all along he meant to betray me?"

Lady Elizabeth was not sufficiently overset to allow such a remark to pass unanswered. "Only an absolute mollycoddle could place her reliance in a man who refused to be received by her family. It seems to me that you have allowed some foolish notions of girlish romance to bring scandal upon us all."

Georgiana intervened hastily, before the Viscount could perceive the justice of Lady Elizabeth's remarks.

"Oh, Aunt Elizabeth, I'm so sorry! I did not plan to do anything wrong, indeed I did not. But when I was told that I was to marry Freddie, I'm afraid that I practised a little deception. I only pretended to be grateful for your kindness in arranging such a splendid match for me, and then as soon as I could I left a message for the Marquis to meet me at our usual rendezvous in the woods. And I told him everything. He promised to help me. He said . . ." Here Georgiana's voice became lost in sobs and tiny tears chased down her cheeks. She looked across at the Marquis, inwardly quaking at the utter rigidity of his body and the violence that she suspected lurked very close to the surface.

"Oh, Julian, how could you do this?" She caught his eye and her voice trembled most convincingly. "You said that we should be married in your chapel. You told me that you had a special licence and that I had only to come with you and all my problems would be over. Now we come back here and I discover you are a deceiver. How could you betray me so?"

Georgiana's composure was finally broken, and she fell back against the cushions of her chair in a storm of weeping. Her godfather spoke sternly over the awful noise. "Would you be good enough to ring for your maid, Lady Elizabeth? It is clear that my poor goddaughter has strayed, but she is overcome and her punishment must be postponed for the time being. She is in urgent need of rest."

Not for nothing had the Viscount helped organise one of the most complicated and successful peace treaties in the history of Europe. His orders rolled impressively from his tongue. "My dear Lady Elizabeth, you too must be in need of a period of quiet repose. The Marquis and I will continue our discussion once my godchild is safely in her bedchamber. You will wish to inform Lord Thayne of what has occurred, and we shall no doubt have some further news to convey to him very shortly." He handed Georgiana his handkerchief.

"My dear child, you must calm yourself. I have been a busy man in recent years and I think I have failed in my duty to your father, who was an old and cherished friend. I can safely leave your aunt to point out to you the moral wickedness of your actions, but you may rely upon me to salvage what we can from the consequences of your folly. You, after all, are no more than a young and inexperienced girl. The Marquis of Graydon is a man of the world, several years your senior. He knows what course of action he must take if he wishes to be accounted a man of honour."

Georgiana, who was rapidly developing a case of very genuine hysterics as she began to realise the terrible consequences of her almost frivolous attempt at revenge, murmured her thanks. Viscount Benham was proving too kind for her peace of mind, and even her aunt was showing disconcerting symptoms of genuine sorrow rather than mere malice towards the Marquis. As for the Marquis of Graydon, one look at his silent and brooding figure was sufficient to convince Georgiana that it was safer not to consider his probable reactions at all.

She hardly needed to simulate relief when a footman finally returned escorting Marguerite, and it was almost no pretence at all when she clung with shaky hands to the strong support of Marguerite's arm. As personal maid to Lady Elizabeth, Marguerite had not felt at all pleased when summoned to assist the wretched and dowdy Miss Thayne, but the girl's case was so obviously desperate that even her proud spirit relented slightly and she mouthed soothing platitudes all the way up the stairs and into Miss Thayne's rooms. If she was astonished at the change in her charge's face and figure she made no comment upon it, simply helping Miss Thayne into fresh clothes, tidying her hair and leaving her to recline upon a comfortable chaise-longue in front of the bedroom fire.

Georgiana was in a state bordering upon nervous collapse, and allowed Marguerite to clothe her, wash her and dress her hair without uttering a single word. Her mind seemed entirely blank, the events of the past few days blotted out in a black haze of panic. The image of the Marquis' face as she had last seen him constantly impressed itself on her mind, and she found herself silently repeating, over and over again, "What have I done? I think he may kill me, what have I done?"

CHAPTER
EIGHT

By dinner time, Georgiana had managed to get her fears under slightly better and more rational control. She was not optimistic enough to imagine that the Marquis would ever forgive her for the outrageous tissue of lies she had invented; on the other hand, she was beginning to feel that what she had done was not so very bad in view of the fact that the Marquis had always intended to use her as an innocent pawn in his highly devious plots.

At first she was grateful that everybody in the household seemed to be leaving her severely alone. A light luncheon was brought to her room by a young kitchen-maid who was far too frightened at being above-stairs to contemplate speaking to any of the august personages she encountered in the course of her deliveries. Georgiana, in fact, was so lost in her own speculations that she hardly noticed who had entered her room, and was astonished when the same maid returned to remove her empty tray since she had no memory of having eaten anything.

By late afternoon, however, her solitude was beginning to pall. Georgiana was attempting to decide whether it was better to stay in her room and avoid unpleasant confrontations, or get dressed for dinner and at least resolve some of the unanswered questions swirling around in her head, when Marguerite arrived in the doorway with a message from her aunt.

"Lady Elizabeth says you are to join the rest of the family for dinner, Miss Thayne. And she says she hopes you are by now over the hysterics. She has more than enough to put up with tonight without you going off into floods of tears every time anybody looks at you."

Marguerite, well aware that Lady Elizabeth had expected her irritable message to be considerably toned down by the time it was delivered, looked at Miss Thayne with a hint of malice. There were obviously mysterious and nefarious doings afoot, and Marguerite's professional pride had been touched on the raw when she realised that Miss Thayne had been systematically deceiving the entire household about her looks and her figure. Glancing sharply at the tall, composed young woman who now stood in front of her, Marguerite was hard put to believe that this was the same dowdy frump who had defeated her highly-trained dressing skills time and time again. Moreover, Marguerite sensed that even the wretched girl's manner was now infinitely more assured, despite the fine turmoil that her absence had created among the other members of the household.

Georgiana looked at Marguerite's rigidly hostile figure and allowed a wry smile to touch her lips. "Thank you for delivering my aunt's message so – accurately, Marguerite. Since I am to join my family for dinner, perhaps you would help me to select the least voluminous of my gowns? You will see that I have slippers and gloves already chosen. My hair, too, will need a little of your attention."

"Very good, Miss Thayne." Reluctantly, Marguerite moved over to the large armoire, filled with dresses that were quite useless to Miss Thayne with her present figure. Gradually, Marguerite's professional pride –

which was very great – overcame all other feelings, and a stirring of excitement quickened her eye as she ran it over the rack of gowns.

She finally extracted a dress of white gauze spangled with silver that had been monstrously unsuitable when worn by the old, exceedingly plump, Miss Thayne. From the bottom of one of the chests she extracted a thin silk petticoat which Georgiana recognised as dating from the early days after her father's death. It was simple in style as befitted a very young girl, and far too skimpy to fit over the padding that Georgiana had habitually assumed. The petticoat was therefore almost unworn and smelled softly of the lavender sachets under which it had been stored. Georgiana allowed the maid to slip the petticoat over her head and stood uncomplainingly while Marguerite smoothed the silver gauze overdress tightly across the bodice, snipping the excess fabric with her tiny scissors and sewing minute seams with the nimbleness of skilful fingers.

When she had finished her work the skirt of the gown remained fuller than fashion dictated, but the soft folds of transparent fabric were rather becoming and Georgiana felt a modest satisfaction with her appearance. Whatever uproar she might have to face tonight, at least she would face it looking reasonably well-groomed. After so many years of dowdiness, this was not a pleasure to be altogether despised.

Marguerite finished sweeping Georgiana's hair high on her head, leaving the long column of her neck quite bare. Georgiana removed diamond ear-drops from her jewellery case. They were perhaps a little ostentatious for a county dinner, but it was hard to resist emphasizing the delicate line of her cheeks. "I shall not wear any other jewellery, Marguerite. Thank you for helping me so expertly with my gown – I am grateful to you for an excellent job."

Marguerite looked in silence at her handiwork, and for a short while Georgiana feared that she was still too offended to speak. Slowly the maid shook her head.

"You look beautiful, Miss Thayne, and I was blind not to see it before. Why ever did you . . ." Hastily she recollected herself. "If you would care to select a day-dress from your wardrobe, ma'am, I should be happy to see that it is adjusted for you. It will take time to arrange for new gowns to be made, even though we are fortunate enough to have the new supplies of muslin and silk that Lady Elizabeth brought back from Bristol."

Georgiana smiled a little shyly. "Why, of course! My wedding trousseau, I had forgotten." The reminder of Lady Elizabeth and the wrath still to come was not at all pleasant, and she sighed. "I am glad you perceive a change for the better in my looks, Marguerite, and it is kind of you to suggest the alterations. It would certainly be most helpful to have something a little smaller to wear. Here." Swiftly she removed two of her simplest dresses from the closet. "These seem to have fewer furbelows than the rest. Perhaps you can make something a bit more in style from them while we are waiting for the dressmaker to complete her work."

Marguerite took the dresses, curtsied and went out of the room, casting one final and obviously approving look at the results of her handiwork. Lady Elizabeth was a handsome matron who took good care of her face and figure, but there was certainly more pleasure to be drived from dressing a really beautiful young woman.

Georgiana herself lingered a while longer in front of the looking-glass, her expression troubled as she con-templated the endless discussion that her vastly altered appearance was likely to generate. The tangled web of deception was certainly closing in upon her with increasingly strong threads. Reluctantly she acknowledged that she could delay her descent no longer, and just as she walked hesitantly to the door a footman knocked politely in order to remind her that the hour for dinner was now long past. He managed to maintain the blank expression so prized by superior servants as Georgiana walked past him into the corridor, but his eyes betrayed an admiring astonishment that lifted Georgiana's spirits as it simultaneously increased her nervous anticipation of the evening ahead.

As soon as she arrived at the entrance to the large salon where everybody had gathered to await dinner, Georgiana realised that she had made a grave tactical error in leaving her entry so late. The rest of the household had obviously been chattering idly while waiting with various degrees of impatience to proceed into the dining room, but as soon as her presence was noticed a stunned silence fell upon the assembled group. Like the actors in a drama who expect the fall of the curtain, her family and their guest seemed frozen in postures of arrested animation. Only their eyes moved, tracing the outline of her face and her figure with silent wonder.

Georgiana herself felt quite incapable of movement, scarcely even able to identify the ranks of hostile observers as individuals. Her brain was paralysed by embarrassment and she was able to do no more than stand silent, her hand hovering over the door-handle, wondering if she looked as grotesquely startled as the remaining occupants of the room.

Finally Lady Elizabeth broke the spell by moving commandingly towards the dining salon, almost ignoring Georgiana as she swept past her. "We shall leave discussion of these serious matters until after dinner. But, Viscount Benham, I must tell you here and now that I consider your plans for Georgiana's future highly unsuitable. We have nourished a viper in the bosom of our family, and I personally feel that only a prolonged period of solitary prayer and mediation is suitable treatment for a young girl who has erred so profoundly."

Viscount Benham, who prior to this majestic speech had been thinking that his god-daughter owed him a long explanation of the various deceits and subterfuges that had clearly been practised within the Thayne family, was instantly upon the defensive.

"My god-daughter, Lady Elizabeth, is now twenty-two years of age and wishes to marry a man who is her equal in birth and breeding and who is, moreover, your nearest neighbour. In the circumstances – in view of the regrettable failure to have my god-daughter presented at the proper time – I feel we may all congratulate ourselves that her affairs are to be settled with so little likelihood of causing public comment. I shall speak to Georgiana after dinner as you have suggested, and point out to her the foolishness of entering into a secret engagement with a man who could not gain the full approval of her family."

The Viscount was striding across the hallway, the remainder of the family trailing attentively in his wake. He cast a glance over his shoulder and added sternly, "I suggest we spend our time at dinner discussing useful matters such as the arrangements it will be necessary for me to make in order to take Georgiana back to town with me when I leave next week. I understand that the Marquis of Graydon wishes to make the announcement of his betrothal in London before the Season is over."

And having delivered himself of this startling speech, the Viscount looked round the table at the assembled group of Thaynes, well satisfied with the absolute stupefaction visible on every face.

It was Freddie who found his voice first. Lady Elizabeth and Georgiana were – for different reasons – only too grateful to sink into the chairs thoughtfully pulled out for them by the attendant footmen.

"But I say, my lord, Georgie can't marry that fellow Graydon. I mean to say, dash it all, she's engaged to me!"

Freddie was feeling peeved. He had agreed to marry Georgiana even when she had seemed a dowdy frump. Now she had turned into a ravishing beauty, and suddenly his new-found prize was about to be snatched from him. "Can't be betrothed to two men at once, you know." He looked pleased with this expression of indisputable social wisdom. "And she's engaged to me, so stands to reason she can't be engaged to that fellow Graydon."

"Do stop saying 'that fellow Graydon'," said Lady Elizabeth with extreme irritation.

Lord Thayne saw that the moment had arrived for him to exert his titular authority as head of the house, and he cleared his throat in a ponderous manner. He look reprovingly at his son. "Benham and I have already settled the whole matter with that fellow . . . that is to say, we have settled it with the Marquis of Graydon that the irregular nature of his meeting with Georgie is to be forgiven, since he has agreed to marry her with all possible speed. I shall discuss the matter with you and with your mother after dinner. Viscount Benham, as Georgiana's godfather, has already told you that he is taking upon himself the responsibility of explaining his arrangements to Georgiana. You, Freddie, must do your best to control your disappointment."

His unnaturally pontifical manner deserted him as he caught his son's aggrieved eye. "For heaven's sake, Freddie, don't kick up such a dust over nothing. Two days ago you were telling me you wouldn't marry the girl as a gift. Now you're telling me she can't marry anybody else because she's engaged to you. You could have had her any time these past four years with my blessing. Now somebody else has chosen to take her off our hands, and that's an end to it as far as I'm concerned."

Georgiana, appalled by the sequence of vulgarities in her uncle's exposition of her future, was nevertheless relieved to see that Freddie at last was silenced. Lady Elizabeth retreated into an outraged and icy formality, uttering bare courtesies to the Viscount – who after all was too important a man to be completely ignored, however unworthy his behaviour in regard to Georgiana – and entirely ignoring the other people seated around the dinner table. Georgiana was so used to being either in disgrace, or the object of cold silences, that she found her dinner less disturbed than others at the table. In fact, she was so busily occupied in planning the excuses she would make at her next meeting with the Marquis that she was hard put to pay any attention to such desultory efforts at conversation as did occur.

After the departure of the ladies, Lord Thayne and his son consumed brandy with the steady dedication of confirmed drinkers anxious to escape reminder of an unpleasant scene. Viscount Benham soon realised that he was not expected to sustain even a pretence of polite conversation, and he was only recalled from a silent speculation on the probable composition of the next Cabinet when his host regretfully – and very loudly – declined a fifth serving of brandy. With the expression of a martyr performing his most painful duty, Baron Thayne pushed his chair away from the table and stood on passably steady legs.

"If you have finished, Benham," he said, "perhaps you would explain everything to Georgie. We'd better make sure that she understands the wedding will have to take place soon. Can't risk word of what happened leaking out and having it spread all over town."

The Viscount looked at his host with some dislike, and marvelled afresh at the difference between this Lord Thayne and his late brother.

"I am sure we can rely upon you and Freddie to remain silent," said Viscount Benham, "and I hardly think that the Marquis is going to be foolish enough to spread rumours that can only harm the reputation of the woman whom he has chosen to become his wife." He looked severely at the baron. "I agree with you that Georgiana should be settled with all possible speed, but my reasons differ from your own. Now that she is twenty-two, I feel Georgiana is entitled to her own establishment, and I shall be happy to see her respectably married before I leave on another mission for our Government."

The Viscount managed to look hard-pressed and weighted down by the cares of governing the world. In actual fact he was thinking that making treaties with the Prussians was child's play in comparison to marrying off a god-daughter.

Freddie broke impatiently into the slight silence that followed Viscount Benham's remarks. "Well, sir," he addressed his father, "if you don't need me here any more I'll go and make arrangements for posting back to town. I have several appointments I really should be keeping." He thought with intense longing of his ballerina, who was as silly as she was good-natured and always managed to make him feel that he was a splendid gentleman. At least now his parents had no excuse for keeping him away from town and his father admitted as much.

"Well, my boy, we won't delay you. We understand that it would be difficult for you to hang around watching Georgie get ready to marry another man. I expect I'll see you in town some time next week."

Freddie bade a brief farewell to Viscount Benham which left some doubt in the minds of each as to who was more relieved to be bidding goobye to whom. Freddie then retreated through the dining salon doors almost at a gallop, sending urgent instructions to the kitchen quarters for his valet. Only the absence of a full moon prevented him from insisting on having the horses set to, so that he might accomplish the first stage of the journey to London before bedtime. He retired early to bed, anxious to be away at dawn, thus avoiding the unpleasant possibility of a confrontation with his formidable Mamma. He fell asleep heartily cursing all relatives, especially female cousins who spend five years looking absolutely dowdy and then turn into ravishing women just when it is too late to decide to marry them.

CHAPTER
NINE

GEORGIANA had meanwhile endured the longest and most severe scolding that her aunt had ever seen fit to administer. Georgiana had extensive experience of Lady Elizabeth's powers of vituperative admonishment, but on this particular occasion her aunt excelled herself. In fact, so busy was Lady Elizabeth in enumerating the many faults, the examples of base ingratitude, and the premonitions of disaster that Georgiana's behaviour had always aroused, that she quite forgot to demand an adequate explanation either for Georgiana's secret friendship with the Marquis of Graydon, or for her years of masquerade. This happy state of affairs was brought to an abrupt end by the arrival of the tea-tray. Even under the direst of provocations, Lady Elizabeth never betrayed unbecoming emotion in front of the servants, so she was forced to halt her flood of recrimination. Once engaged in her mundane task of pouring out cups of tea, her attention was forcibly recalled to the extraordinary change in her niece's appearance.

When Georgiana moved gracefully from the sofa to accept her tea from Lady Elizabeth and then went to stand, in an attitude betokening slight impatience, in front of the drawing-room windows, it was quite impossible to ignore the fact that the changes in Georgiana's manner and bearing almost exceeded the

changes in her face and figure. With the greatest difficulty, Lady Elizabeth waited until the butler had with-
drawn from the room and then she looked at her niece
across a bosom heaving with emotion.

"Well, Georgiana, I am waiting to hear your explanation for this disgraceful escapade. I would also like to
know *exactly* why you found it necessary to deceive
your family as to your true appearance. I am almost
afraid to enquire what further scandal you have been
plunging us all into, whilst hiding behind that mask of
infantile simplicity. It is intolerable that you should
have chosen to betray the trust of the people who were
good enough to care for you when your father died."

Recalling that Georgiana's financial position was
such that disinterested observers might consider that
Georgiana had been caring for her uncle and aunt rather
than the other way around, Lady Elizabeth quickly
reverted to the main thrust of her argument. "Yes,
well, I am still waiting for an explanation of your deception, Georgiana."

Georgiana cast about wildly in her mind to think of
some plausible reason for the highly improbable state of
affairs that had existed at Thayne Hall for so long. It
suddenly occurred to her that deception had become so
much a part of her habit of mind that she no longer
considered telling her aunt the truth. But the moment
for honesty seemed finally to have arrived, so she
turned and looked at her aunt very directly.

"I adopted that foolish disguise, Aunt Elizabeth,
because I needed to conceal any feminine attractions
that I may have. I was afraid you and my uncle would
coerce me into marriage with my cousin, so I tried to
make sure that Freddie would feel as much opposed to
the match as I do myself. I did not wish to marry

Freddie when I was sixteen, and I still do not wish to marry him – we should make one another most unhappy." She smiled rather bitterly. "Of course the disguise that I adopted was childish, but then the plan was thought up by me when I was scarcely more than a child. And you will understand how once the deception was started it became increasingly difficult to think how I might bring it to a halt. I cannot apologise for the subterfuge I have practised towards you and my uncle. I believe I feel too much resentment that such subterfuge was necessary."

As she spoke the incredible words of defiance, Georgiana trembled with indefinable emotion now that the long years of pretence were finally over. She realised in those few moments what an enormous burden the constant acting of a lie had become. Speaking the truth had magically liberated her from bonds that had recently become suffocating. Whatever else happened as a result of the Marquis' abduction, she would always have to be grateful to him that his actions had finally precipitated this confrontation. Georgiana hoped very much that Lady Elizabeth would lose her temper completely and cast her off, thus leaving Georgiana free to seek out her governess and retire to an independent establishment – a dream that Georgiana had long since despaired of fulfilling. Visions of a small country house with a cozy cottage garden flashed into the mind's eye, and she turned away from her aunt in order to conceal the intense longing for tranquillity that suddenly filled her being.

"Your wickedness," replied Lady Elizabeth, "surpasses even my worst imaginings. Do not think that your godfather will believe these extraordinary statements of yours! When have your uncle and I ever attempted to force you into marriage with our son? Only two nights ago you expressed the utmost delight because your uncle had suggested the marriage to you. Now you are asking me to believe that for six years you have adopted a preposterous disguise simply in order to avoid a marriage that was never proposed to you until recently, and which then appeared to send you into transports of happiness."

Lady Elizabeth's cold voice hardened still further. "I should be at a loss to understand where your powers of deception sprang from if I had not discovered your dreadful liaison with the Marquis of Graydon. Painful as it is for me to mention his name, I have only to contemplate his involvement in this affair to understand the reason for all your wicked actions. The man is undoubtedly a monster whose viciousness is exceeded only by his fatal attraction for foolish girls." Her face softened into a smile. "Not that my dear sister Chloë was foolish, but she was young and in those days the Marquis was careful to conceal his vices from public view."

It was impossible for Lady Elizabeth to sit still any longer. Rage consumed her and she turned in fury to face her niece. "But you! You have no excuse. You must have heard that his name is anathema to me. You probably even knew of the way in which my poor Chloë died. And yet you could still deceive us all – meeting him secretly, whilst I believed you still innocent, almost a child!"

Georgiana felt a reluctant sympathy. Her aunt's distress was disturbingly genuine. "Oh no! It wasn't as you imagine, Aunt Elizabeth. There has been a dreadful misunderstanding, and my involvement with the Marquis is not quite as it seems . . ."

"Do not attempt to overcome my opposition with your wiles, Georgiana. I will not permit that man to enter my house, so if you are intending to persist with this utterly scandalous betrothal it is perhaps as well that your godfather has seen fit to announce that he is taking you to London. Do not expect me to give you countenance when the Marquis abandons you – as he undoubtedly will. No woman has managed to trap him into matrimony since he realised what he lost in my dear Chloë, and he certainly couldn't be expected to change his pattern for a silly young thing like you, even if you have got a better face and figure than any of us suspected!"

Georgiana felt herself at an absolute loss to answer her aunt, and it was with visible relief that she saw the door opening to admit her godfather and her uncle. Viscount Benham cast one look at the two distraught women and stepped nobly into the breach.

"Georgiana, perhaps you would be good enough to accompany me into your uncle's study. I am sure that Lord Thayne would enjoy some minutes of private conversation with Lady Elizabeth, and I have several matters to discuss with you." He saw that his god-daughter still looked considerably chastened and he added soothingly, "We must also make haste to set in train the arrangements for your departure to London. The Marquis of Graydon awaits your arrival with some impatience."

"You cannot mean the Marquis of Graydon has already left for London!" Georgiana was horror-struck. Viscount Benham chuckled patronisingly, confident that he understood the reason for Georgiana's concern. "Never fear, my dear. The Marquis asked me to convey to you his apologies for his abrupt departure – and it will not be many days before you are reunited. Afraid he'll forget all about you once he's back in the busy city, eh?"

"No," Georgiana answered despairingly, "that was not precisely what I was worried about."

Lady Elizabeth, who had listened to this exchange in stony silence, now gave every evidence of girding her loins preparatory to launching a fresh verbal attack, and the Viscount threw only one hasty look in her direction before speaking firmly to his god-daughter.

"Come along, Georgiana. It is getting late and I must talk to you before the evening is quite over."

Georgiana sat meekly in the library waiting for Viscount Benham to settle himself in a comfortable chair with a glass of wine. The calm she had maintained so precariously throughout dinner was now quite dissipated, for she had never supposed that the Marquis of Graydon would remove himself from the neighbourhood without demanding the opportunity to speak privately with her. How was she to offer the Marquis explanations for her actions if he was already seventy miles distant? Nervously she shredded the sad remnants of a once fine lace handkerchief and Viscount Benham, remarking her distress, patted her soothingly on the arm.

"Now, Georgiana," he said, "you must not be frightened of me. You were brought up by your parents to understand the highest moral principles, so you do not need a scolding from me to remind you that in meeting the Marquis of Graydon clandestinely you have been behaving most reprehensibly. It is not to be wondered at if Lady Elizabeth finds herself distinctly out of humour with you. After all, you have been committed to her charge for some years, and such behaviour must reflect adversely upon her.

"However," he smiled at Georgiana quite kindly, "I have no doubt your aunt has already said more than enough to you on that subject, and the Marquis has explained to me that there was originally no thought of an elopement on your part."

Georgiana turned startled blue eyes upon her godfather. "Yes," Viscount Benham continued, "he has told me that you looked upon him as a friend and counsellor in a difficult . . . family . . . situation here at Thayne Hall. He explained to me that you went only to seek his advice in the matter of your impending betrothal to Freddie, and that the idea of a secret marriage was his alone."

The Viscount stood up and adopted the commanding posture that had proved so successful when negotiating with recalcitrant foreigners. "It is regrettable, Georgiana, that you allowed yourself to be swayed by the Marquis into agreeing to such an unmaidenly act, but Graydon has acknowledged the major part of the blame to be his. Fortunately for us all he is prepared to stand by the consequences of his rashness, and has been most accommodating in agreeing to hasten the marriage between you."

Georgiana continued to look more cowed than the Viscount altogether wished, so he cleared his throat in some embarrassment. "I have a confession to make." He smiled at Georgiana with a wry blend of charm and unfeigned humility. "I sometimes exaggerate the amount of work I do for the government in order to avoid unpleasant obligations of a trivial nature. But believe me, my dear, I have never willingly shirked my responsibilities to you. On the contrary, I am full of guilt because I have so often felt it necessary to put the needs of our country before my duties towards you.

The consequences of my unavoidable neglect have not been happy."

He stopped speaking, and Georgiana immediately rose and went to stand near the Viscount, resting her hand gently on his velvet sleeve. "Indeed, sir," she said, "even in the midst of so much family drama I hope I am able to retain some sense of proportion. I understand how very important your work at the Congress of Vienna has been in bringing matters to a successful conclusion." She gave a small laugh. "There have been one or two black days, of course, when I felt that the fate of Europe was as nothing in comparison to the woes of my position here at Thayne Hall, but I assure you that a brisk walk down to the village and a pleasant afternoon spent chatting to Miss Harris, soon restored my sense of perspective. It *was* a great relief to us both when we heard that you had finally returned to London for a prolonged visit, and we did hope that you would find time to put my affairs in order – but we didn't begrudge your services to the government more than once or twice a week!"

"Well, now your affairs are in order." The Viscount smiled with relief that his burden of guilt could be discarded. "I was aware from the time of my arrival here that you did not particularly wish to marry your cousin, but I'm afraid that Lord Thayne's trusteeship of your inheritance has been . . . in short, I found myself placed in somewhat of a dilemma. And I regret to say that under the pressure of considering new instructions constantly issuing from the Foreign Secretary's office, I was happy to relegate your personal problems to a low level of priority."

Georgiana made a tiny gesture of reassurance, and the Viscount sipped his wine contentedly and heaved a small sigh of relief. "There is no doubt that Graydon has behaved handsomely over all this. It is not every prospective bridegroom who would be as willing as the Marquis to overlook the – irregularities – in the settlements we shall be making at the time of your marriage."

The Viscount disliked having to think about the unpleasant shortages in his god-daughter's inheritance, so he moved the conversation on to more agreeable topics. "I don't know what the Marquis had been saying to Lady Elizabeth just before I came into the room this morning, but it is quite clear that you had mistaken his intentions, my dear. Once his arrangements for an immediate secret marriage had fallen through, he never had any plan other than to return you safely to your family and to beg for permission to regularise the regrettable situation that had arisen between you."

Georgiana was rendered speechless by the audacity of her supposed fiancé. Rapidly her mind reviewed the possible reasons for his actions. Was he hoping for the payment of some huge sum of money, perhaps from Georgiana herself? Or was it conceivable that he had actually decided to go through with the marriage – seizing the opportunity presented by her own actions to get his hands on a comfortable fortune?

Georgiana suppressed a bitter laugh. No wonder he was behaving with such nobility over the settlements! Why should a man who was desperately in need of money quibble because his bride-to-be was bringing in a dowry of only fifty thousand pounds, instead of the seventy thousand pounds rumour credited her with?

But of course she could tell none of this to her god-father, because the Marquis – however disreputable his motives – still represented her only possible escape route from the suffocating future offered by continued residence at Thayne Hall. And buried somewhere inside her, so deeply that she was not willing to acknowledge its existence, was the conviction that marriage to the Marquis, whatever his vices, was infinitely to be preferred to marriage with Freddie, whatever his hidden virtues. So she smiled at her godfather and said simply, "I am grateful to you, sir, for all that you have done for me today. Now tell me, when do you wish to leave for town?"

The Viscount laughed drily. "I *wish* to leave for town tomorrow morning. I realise that such an early departure would be quite impossible for you, however, since you will undoubtedly have many arrangements to make." He paused for a minute and tried to think what arrangements any unattached female could possibly have to make and could conceive of none. Nevertheless, years of experience warned him that his goddaughter would undoubtedly start to bore him with the details of the changes needed in her wardrobe and the list of friends to whom it was imperative for her to bid farewell if he gave her the opportunity, so he spoke quickly. "Do you think we could count on leaving first thing on Monday morning? I really cannot absent myself from town much longer than that."

Georgiana thought of all the sewing and packing that would have to be done in order to send her to London even modestly equipped, but she smiled brightly and said, "Oh yes, I'm sure we shall manage to be ready. May I ask where you are planning for me to stay?"

"My widowed sister, Lady Vaudon, acts as hostess for me whenever I am in England. It will therefore be perfectly proper for you to stay in my house, and I am relying upon my sister to see that you are presented to the people who should have been made known to you years ago."

Unhappily aware that he had been guilty of implicitly criticising his hostess, the Viscount allowed his voice to tail away into silence. Georgiana interjected with deliberate brightness, "May I ask Miss Harris to accompany me? I am sure Lady Vaudon will have many engagements, and it would relieve her of some wearisome duties if my former governess were available to accompany me."

The Viscount beamed with delight. "Now that is an excellent notion. My sister is not precisely energetic, and she will be relieved to find her duties nominal rather than actual. Admiring the cathedrals of London would undoubtedly be more in Miss Harris' line than in Adelaide's."

"I shall certainly want to see all the famous sights," announced Georgiana. "I have never before travelled further than Bath, so this trip will be a great treat for me."

"Quite apart from all the excitement of seeing your betrothed again, eh?" The Viscount looked at Georgiana's downcast eyes and teased her gently. "Ah, you girls are all the same! Determined to fall in love and cast all your elders' sensible plans into confusion. You'd better go along to bed now and dream of your handsome Marquis, otherwise your aunt will be coming in to find out if I've finished scolding you."

Georgiana decided not to attempt to disabuse her godfather of any of his misapprehensions and retired gracefully to bed. If she did happen to dream of the Marquis, she thought bitterly, it was quite likely to be a nightmare. Dark eyes and a cynical mouth forced their way into her mind and with a bad-tempered pull of the bell-rope, Georgiana summoned the maid who would help her to bed. The alarms and excursions of this particular day had lasted quite long enough.

CHAPTER
TEN

THE travelling coach had rumbled and jolted over the tuurnpike for almost eleven hours, and finally the seventy miles separating Thayne Hall from London were completed. Miss Harris and Georgiana got down from the carriage, weary from the miles of constant motion, but excited by the noise and activity all around them. Viscount Benham, well used to the sights, sounds and smells of London, strode impatiently across the pavement and rapped on the door of an impressive house. It was immediately opened and a pleasantly bright light streamed out, piercing the gathering darkness of the misty spring evening. Georgiana, feeling very much the country cousin, walked up to the porticoed entrance and obtained her first glimpse of a London mansion. She cast a nervous glance at the butler, was pleased to discover that he looked very similar to every other butler she had ever seen, and managed to decide that the entrance hall looked astonishingly narrow before she was ushered by Viscount Benham into a large salon, furnished in the very latest fashions.

Reclining – it was impossible to pretend that the figure was sitting – in front of the fire on a straw satin sofa was a lady of truly awesome proportions. Dressed in an outfit that to Georgiana's inexperienced eyes seemed more suitable to the boudoir than the drawing room, she raised a languid arm in greeting. Diamond bracelets shimmered among the rolls of flesh and a mound of satin-covered bosom was surmounted by an array of red, blue and green jewels. The huge stones winked on the huge bosom, and Georgiana blinked in disbelief.

The Viscount, obviously well accustomed to his sister's bizarre appearance, paid no attention to her state of semi-déshabillée, and introduced Georgiana and Miss Harris with calm good manners. "Adelaide, this is my god-daughter, Miss Thayne, and her companion, Miss Harris." Dutifully Georgiana performed a slight curtsey. "Georgiana, Miss Harris, this is my sister, Lady Adelaide Vaudon. She will be happy to help you make whatever arrangements are necessary before the wedding."

It was evident that the Viscount now considered his duties as a guardian over, for he sketched the briefest of bows in the direction of his ward and her companion before leaving the room, muttering over his shoulder that he must change before calling on Lord Carringdon and bringing himself up to date on affairs in Vienna.

Lady Vaudon still had not uttered a word, but she watched the Viscount rush out of the doors before saying to the room at large, "Lord, what an exhausting man." She then relapsed into her former state of total lethargy, and Georgiana regarded her in quiet despair for several minutes before venturing to ask if they might retire to their rooms. Lady Vaudon heaved herself up into a sitting position, a task of no mean magnitude in view of her enormous bulk and clinging draperies.

"Your rooms?" she enquired without ill-humour but

with obvious astonishment. "Are you expecting to stay here?"

Miss Harris blushed bright pink. "Lady Vaudon, did the Viscount not send somebody ahead to let you know that we were coming? Georgiana and I are expecting to stay here for some weeks."

Lady Vaudon thought long and silently. Georgiana, her body aching from the hours in the coach, made the sad discovery that conversation with Lady Vaudon proceeded at an unbearably lethargic pace. Finally Lady Vaudon shook her head regretfully.

"I expect that was the message George brought me this afternoon. I quite forgot to read it." She smiled confidingly at Miss Harris. "When Benham is in town I am incredibly efficient. I read all my correspondence and get up every morning well before noon. But you see, he was out of town. And when my brother is out of town I have a little holiday." She smiled happily. "Never mind. Our housekeeper is marvellous, she will have everything ready for you in a trice. You, the young one, what's your name? Ring the bell over there will you, please, and ask the housekeeper to come here."

Georgiana did as she was bid, not bothering to repeat her name, which she was confident would only be forgotten again. The housekeeper appeared shortly, looking remarkably sane and even-tempered for a person who no doubt had to cope with all the consequences of Lady Vaudon's overwhelming lassitude. Lady Vaudon smiled sweetly and said simply, "We need two rooms prepared for our guests." A sudden thought struck her, and she turned back to her visitors. "Have you travelled far? Do you wish for some refreshments?"

"We have journeyed from Thayne Hall," said Georgiana. "Your brother has been a guest of my uncle and aunt. It has been a long day and we should be grateful for something to eat if it would be possible to have something in our rooms."

She spoke quite firmly, for she had decided that delicate hints were not likely to penetrate the rolls of flesh encasing Lady Vaudon's mind. The housekeeper, not bothering to wait for an answer that might never come, promised Georgiana that bedchambers and food would be ready within a few minutes. "Palmer, the butler, told us that you had brought a fair bit of luggage, ma'am, so we knew that rooms would be needed, and my maids have been putting things to rights almost since the carriage drew up at the door. If you would like to wait here with Lady Vaudon, Palmer will tell you when your bedchambers are prepared."

Lady Vaudon crunched delicately on a macaroon, and sighed happily as the housekeeper left the room. "Benham has such marvellous servants. I don't know how we should go on without them all."

Georgiana, who had not eaten since lunchtime, eyed the dish of macaroons with considerable longing and bit back all of the scathing answers that flashed into her mind. Poor Miss Harris was looking exhausted, and entirely ill at ease in the presence of an eccentric well beyond the scope of a social life previously limited to Thayne Village and the outskirts of Bath. Georgiana and Miss Harris were both too exhausted to make the supreme effort of initiating conversation with Lady Vaudon, so silence reigned uneasily in the room until Lady Vaudon's voice broke into the hush.

"Where did you get that sketch of a gown?"

Georgiana thought for one minute that she must have imagined the question, both because Lady Vaudon's expression remained as indolent as ever, and also because even in London such remarks could surely not be considered acceptable drawing-room conversation between virtual strangers. She therefore decided to ignore the words and smiled nervously at Miss Harris, hoping silently but fervently that Palmer's return would not be long delayed.

"I said something." Lady Vaudon's voice sounded aggrieved. She clearly did not expect to make the effort of speaking only to have her conversation ignored. "You, the young one. You're quite a good-looking gal, so why are you wearing that sketch of a gown?"

Fury overcame Georgiana's natural restraint. "Probably for much the same reason that you are wearing that sketch of a negligée. It happens to fit me and *I* thought it was quite presentable."

This hardly seemed the moment to point out that the Thayne Village dressmaker had been called upon to complete five outfits in five days and had worked from fashion plates given to Miss Harris four years previously.

Lady Vaudon looked at Georgiana without a trace of animosity in her expression. Her eyes, however, offered mild reproach. "My dear girl, I have been married twice and have now retired to indulge myself in the ways I never could when I was chasing around proving to everybody that I was a more successful hostess than they were. But you – you haven't even been married once, and you let yourself be seen looking like that!"

"My circumstances have been such that I have had little choice in the matter," said Georgiana stiffly. "Miss Harris and I plan to rectify the omissions in my wardrobe as swiftly as possible."

A faint gleam appeared in Lady Vaudon's languid eye. "Are you shopping on a budget?"

Miss Harris uttered a faint protest. "Lady Vaudon . . . such an unfortunate question . . ."

Georgiana, who by now had taken Lady Vaudon in absolute dislike, smiled her thanks at Miss Harris, but nevertheless replied curtly to Lady Vaudon, "No, I have no particular limit on what I plan to spend."

"Ah!" said Lady Vaudon. "Then I shall dress you."

Georgiana was about to deline this amazing offer politely but very firmly, when Palmer appeared to announce that their rooms were now ready. Georgiana and Miss Harris bade brief goodnights to their hostess, who did incline her head in acknowledgement, before returning to her former posture of total indolence against the cushions of the sofa.

Once safely in the sanctuary of their adjoining rooms, Georgiana and Miss Harris looked at one another in silent wonderment. Georgiana finally burst out laughing. "Oh Harry! There is nothing to do in the circumstances except laugh or have hysterics, and I think I am too tired for hysterics!"

Miss Harris joined in the laughter. "We are certainly enlarging our experience of life very rapidly." She looked round the room appreciatively. "I must say that I agree with Lady Vaudon on one matter. Her brother's servants are outstanding. These rooms are delightfully kept and spotlessly clean. We both, have hot water awaiting us, and warming pans in the bed. If only we could be provided with something to eat and drink, I think I might have courage to face the night ahead and even to hope that tomorrow all might seem quite rational again."

She had hardly finished speaking before a light tap at

the door presaged the arrival of two trays of food.
Georgiana looked at the steaming soup and fresh bread
before smiling at her companion.

"It seems as though your wish has been granted,
Miss Harris. Let's eat, then sleep and see if things may
not look brighter in the morning."

When they awoke on Tuesday, Georgiana and Miss
Harris were encouraged to find the daily routine reas-
suringly normal. A maidservant brought chocolate to
their rooms, together with a message that Viscount
Benham would be waiting to see them at noon. Breakfast was served in one of the parlours shortly before
eleven, and Georgiana heaved a heartfelt sigh of relief
when she and Miss Harris finished eating before Lady
Vaudon stirred from her room. The sun shone from a
blue sky, the street was filled with interesting people,
promenading in a marvellous array of outlandish
clothes, and Georgiana decided that however terrible
her forthcoming interview with the Marquis should
turn out to be, her escape to town compensated for a
great deal of mental anguish.

Viscount Benham, a more impressive figure against
the background of England's capital city than in his
uneasy rôle as a guest in a country house, welcomed
them into his library at noon and placed the resources of
his house at their disposal. A barouche had been made
permanently available to Georgiana and Miss Harris,
and the Viscount urged his guests to visit the many
places of interest so frequently ignored by members of
the *haut ton*.

Miss Harris nodded approvingly and assured the
Viscount that she had already planned a schedule of
visits to all the most important points of cultural and
historical interest. The Viscount listened politely, tried

not to be observed as he glanced at his watch, and remarked that the Marquis of Graydon would be calling upon Georgiana early in the morning. He then dismissed his guests politely but charmingly, leaving Georgiana for the first time with a taste of his consummate skill in handling people with supreme courtesy but ruthless despatch. Miss Harris, Georgiana was amused to note, had no idea that she had been managed and retired from the study murmuring praise for the exquisite manners and kind consideration of their host.

It had been agreed between Georgiana and Miss Harris that however important it might be to view the Elgin Marbles in the British Museum and to sigh over the window from which Charles I had watched preparations for his execution, the purchase of suitable clothes for Georgiana – and at least one new evening gown for Miss Harris – took precedence over all other calls on their time. Dismissed from their interview with Viscount Benham, they had therefore only to decide where they should go in order to obtain the speediest service combined with maximum fashionability.

They were standing in the entrance hall pondering this problem with a distinct lack of progress when their dithery conversation was halted by the sounds of a procession descending from the upper hall. Before their awestruck gaze Lady Vaudon, supported on each arm by a maid, preceded by a footman and followed by the housekeeper, walked slowly down the stairs. Arriving in the hall she remarked in pleased tones, "Ah, I'm glad you're waiting for me. The carriage is already outside."

Georgiana spoke hastily. "But Lady Vaudon, we were not aware that you expected us to accompany you.

You sent us no message, and Miss Harris and I therefore intended to do a little shopping."

Lady Vaudon looked at Georgiana with as much impatience as her lethargy was ever likely to enable her to display. "That is why I have made the supreme effort of preparing myself for an outing at this hour of the day. I will take you to my dressmaker."

This remark was almost sufficient to take Georgiana's breath away, but she retained just sufficient composure to say with chilly dignity, "That is very good of you, Lady Vaudon, but Miss Harris and I cannot put you to so much trouble. We shall be quite able to manage a small shopping expedition on our own."

Lady Vaudon, who was far too lazy to indulge in the verbal camouflage that normally passes for polite conversation, looked blandly at Georgiana. "And where are you planning to make your purchases?" she asked baldly.

The question was unfortunately unanswerable, and Miss Harris, who had no more desire than Georgiana to be subjected to an entire afternoon of Lady Vaudon's company, said meekly, "Perhaps you would be good enough to furnish us with the direction of your own *modiste*, then we need trouble you no further?"

Even this suggestion was too much for Georgiana, who looked with horror at her former governess. It was one thing to venture forth into the unknown jungle of London shopping, but quite another to be forced to accept the recommendation of a woman whose taste was as extraordinary as Lady Vaudon's.

"I will take you to Madame Victorine myself," returned Lady Vaudon.

There was nothing that could be done in the face of

such determined civility, and Georgiana seethed silently at the prospect of an entirely wasted afternoon. Her temper was all the more ruffled because she could not admit even to herself that her major interest in the afternoon's shopping had been the purchase of a stunning gown in which to face the Marquis of Graydon. Miss Harris saw her disappointment and cast a glance of mock despair in Georgiana's direction, but they were both too innately courteous to express their opposition more overtly, and they squashed themselves with resignation into the small corner of the carriage that was left free for them by the overflowing curves of Lady Vaudon.

Georgiana spent the first part of the journey staring fixedly out of the carriage window, partly because she wished to bring her annoyance under better control before she ventured some attempt at polite conversation, partly because she wished to orient herself to the various districts of town. She was kind-hearted enough to realise that for a woman of such astonishing indolence, this shopping expedition represented a genuine effort to assist a pair of very green country-dwellers. With a slight sigh, Georgiana mentally acknowledged the generosity of the gesture, while cursing with fluent, silent, but unladylike vigour, the consequences of Lady Vaudon's goodwill.

With her emotions once more under control, she turned back from her contemplation of the passing scene in order to smile at Miss Harris, and glanced up to find Lady Vaudon looking at her with unmistakably malicious humour.

"My taste," said Lady Vaudon, "is superb."

Georgiana inclined her head in polite agreement, but could not quite bring herself to make any more active response. Miss Harris could only look distraught. The silence continued for the length of another street.

"You . . . young lady . . . er . . . Miss Thayne. If you wish to be a success in London you will have to learn to disguise your feelings much more successfully than you can at present manage. Your face tells me plainly that you wish to say that I look outrageous and that therefore my taste is presumably execrable. You are wrong. My taste is superb."

"So you have informed us already." Georgiana was unable to bite off the tart reply before it escaped.

Lady Vaudon examined Georgiana as intently as was possible without making the effort of turning her head. "You will be worth dressing!" she remarked finally and dropped her chin down upon her neck, apparently falling instantly asleep.

"Well, really!" Miss Harris at last recovered use of her tongue. "I must say I find it incredible to believe that Viscount Benham and Lady Vaudon are brother and sister."

Lady Vaudon opened one eye. "It was a great worry to our parents. I was obviously so much more *intelligent* than poor Benham – a dreadful handicap in a daughter who has to be married off. Particularly when she has no looks." She closed her eye and again gave every evidence of being deep in slumber. Miss Harris turned anguished eyes towards Georgiana, then broke into immediate and embarrassed speech.

"I am so looking forward to meeting the Marquis of Graydon again, Georgiana. Such a charming young man. It was tragic when his wife died, and the resulting scandal with Lady Elizabeth . . ."

Miss Harris came to an unhappy halt. Her attempt to cover up one *faux pas* seemed only to have led her into further error. Whatever the reasons for Georgiana's sudden betrothal, Miss Harris was well aware that her pupil was intensely sensitive to any mention of the Marquis' name and remarkably reticent about the sequence of events leading up to her mysterious engagement to the district's most notorious rake. Since she was a woman of good sense, however, Miss Harris made no attempt to gloss over her tactlessness. "I am sorry, Georgiana," she said. "The events of the past few days seem to have deprived me of my wits and certainly of my manners."

Georgiana gave Miss Harris an affectionate pat. "It's hardly your fault, Harry, that every topic of conversation seems to touch upon a subject that offends somebody's sensibilities. One day soon I plan to have a long talk with you and find out why you concealed from me the fact that you knew our Wicked Marquis personally." Miss Harris looked confused and Georgiana smiled slightly. "We shall have a pact, You must tell me all your secrets, and in exchange I shall tell you all of mine."

Miss Harris recovered her dignity. "Well, Georgiana, I am happy to say that I really have nothing more than a few harmless subterfuges to reveal. You sound as if your own disclosures are likely to be considerably more interesting!"

The sudden halting of the carriage fortunately saved Georgiana from the necessity of replying, and the drama of removing Lady Vaudon from the interior of the coach on to the pavement outside the modiste's establishment was sufficently great to banish all other considerations from their minds. Lady Vaudon, who remained entirely unruffled throughout the removal proceedings, was finally escorted into the modish

striped satin workroom of Madame Victorine by two
puffing footmen, a pink-cheeked and flustered Miss
Harris and a regrettably giggling Miss Thayne. Georgiana was surprised to see that the proprietress was
dressed in quiet good taste in a gown of superlative
material and fine workmanship. She was even more
astonished to observe that Madame Victorine accorded
Lady Vaudon every possible consideration, and obviously regarded her presence in the salon as a signal
honour to the establishment.

Lady Vaudon interrupted Madame Victorine's
extensive enquiries into the health of various members
of the Vaudon family with her usual ruthless disregard
for the proprieties.

"We have come to dress this young lady." The puffy
wrist, which today dripped emeralds, was waved vaguely in the direction of Georgiana. Madame Victorine
glanced at Georgiana with cool, professional appraisal.
"Do you, *mademoiselle*, require something in particular?"

Georgiana opened her mouth to suggest that she
might, perhaps, wish to purchase one or two muslin
gowns for morning wear, although she still did not
entirely trust Madame Victorine to produce what she
required. But the words were never uttered.

"She needs everything," said Lady Vaudon. "Her
trousseau. She's marrying Graydon."

Madame Victorine murmured her felicitations and
subjected Georgiana to a second, considerably more
interested, examination. Georgiana meanwhile turned
suspicious eyes towards Lady Vaudon.

"I congratulate you, Lady Vaudon, on the sudden
miraculous improvement of your memory. Yesterday
evening you were scarcely able to remember our names

from moment to moment. But now you remember the name of my fiancé, which surely cannot have been mentioned to you more than once and that, presumably, in a brief conversation with your brother, since I have certainly never discussed my betrothal with you."

The faintest of faint flushes could just be discerned above the ruffles enveloping Lady Vaudon's bosom. "My memory is erratic?" she suggested hopefully.

"I do not doubt it, Lady Vaudon. And it conveniently remembers only those facts which you care to call to mind."

"Georgiana!" Miss Harris conveyed a mild rebuke and Georgiana turned impatiently to Madame Victorine who had been observing the exchange between the clients with superbly feigned indifference.

"For various reasons," said Georgiana, "I have not had the opportunity recently to refurbish my wardrobe. I am in urgent need of some new dresses both for day and evening wear. Could you be of assistance?"

"For Lady Vaudon and her friends we always do our very best," Madame Victorine stated simply. "If you would care to be seated, *mademoiselle*, my assistants will show you some of the fabric we have available in our storerooms. It will be my pleasure to advise you on the way in which the fabrics should be made up – unless Lady Vaudon herself has any suggestions, of course."

Georgiana sank back on the small gilt chair, by now sufficiently bemused to accept that the Lady Vaudon admired by the modiste was not the Lady Vaudon who had half-heartedly extended the hospitality of her brother's house yesterday evening.

In the course of a tiring and beildering afternoon, Georgiana learned that there were indeed at least two Lady Vaudons hiding beneath the corpulent exterior.

Although her visible lethargy did not noticeably diminish, as fabrics were displayed and fashion-plates examined, somehow it was always Lady Vaudon who gave the final judgment on which materials to choose and how best to apply the mutitudinous trimmings. It was Lady Vaudon's languid voice that rejected some models and accepted other until – when exhaustion finally brought Georgiana to a halt – she realised that Lady Vaudon, without ever raising her voice, had indeed selected the entire new wardrobe.

Madame Victorine sent her assistants scurrying off with Georgiana's measurements and profuse assurances that at least one day-dress would be delivered by eight o'clock the following morning. A footman was called and despatched to summon the carriage, while Georgiana turned an exhausted face towards the comfortably recumbent figure of Lady Vaudon. A wry smile twisted her lips.

"Lady Vaudon, I must congratulate you again – but this time most sincerely. A lady who can accomplish what you have done this afternoon without moving from her chair has clearly no need to expend her energies as we lesser mortals must do. Thank you for helping us. Madame Victorine is a pearl beyond price and we could not, of course, have discovered her without your assistance."

Lady Vaudon inclined her head fractionally. "I enjoy selecting clothes," she said, "and you are beautiful."

Georgiana blushed at the compliment, which was obviously sincere since Lady Vaudon would never have wasted breath on mere politeness. Miss Harris, more moderate in her praise, commented contentedly that Georgiana's blue silk evening gown promised to be truly exceptional, and that her own grey satin was quite the most exciting gown she had contemplated wearing for years. In this mood of unexpected contentment and mutual rapport, the three ladies bade goodbye to Madame Victorine and departed from Hanover Square.

CHAPTER
ELEVEN

GEORGIANA had hoped that the arrival of a new gown would improve her appearance sufficiently to bolster her sinking morale, but even as she examined her reflection in the long cheval-glass she resigned herself to failure. No dress, however ravishing, could be expected to calm the storm of nerves which currently afflicted her. The prospect of meeting the Marquis of Graydon was frightening enough to conquer all pleasure in Madame Victorine's sartorial triumph. Even more terrifying than a merely social visit, Viscount Benham had already expressed his intention of allowing Georgiana to spend some time alone with her betrothed. Just to think about this forthcoming private interview threw Georgiana into a fit of nervous fidgets, and she ran her fingers restlessly over the delicately sprigged yellow muslin, wriggling as the abigail attempted for the third time to tie the long ribbons of the satin sash.

"If you could be so good as to stand quite still, Miss, I'd be able to get this finished. I have to do your hair yet and we're never going to be ready."

"I'm sorry," Georgiana apologised meekly and allowed the dresser to get on with her work. Frowning slightly, she took advantage of her enforced immobility to stare at the unknown girl in the mirror.

It had been a mistake, she decided, to place so much

reliance upon the beneficial power of new clothes. Perhaps it was even a mistake to consider testing the effect of her changed appearance at such a difficult moment. The old Miss Thayne was a familiar person, comfortable if not glamorous. This new Miss Thayne, who looked out of the glass with troubled eyes and hesitant expression, was a total stranger of incredible modishness and unknown character. Unable to help herself, Georgiana twitched again impatiently, as if physical movement could cast off her mental uncertainties.

The maid was finally satisfied with her efforts at styling Georgiana's hair, and she stepped back to view her finished product with all the pride of an artist who has completed his ultimate masterpiece. She admired her handiwork for a considerable time and then said, "The gown is wonderfully becoming, Miss, but then I expect you'd look good in anything."

Georgiana flushed faintly with pleasure, then managed a slight laugh. "No," she said. "Not in *anything*. I have it on the impeccable authority of Lady Vaudon that I looked a positive sketch in the gown I wore only two nights ago!"

The maid allowed herself an answering smile. "Oh well, Miss, we all know Lady Vaudon! You've got to be turned out perfect to satisfy her."

Georgiana agreed that Lady Vaudon's standards were severe. "Your name is Susan, is it not?" she asked. The girl nodded. "Thank you for your help, Susan," said Georgiana. "You may go now. I think with your assistance I am quite ready."

Miss Harris and the Viscount waited for her in the library, normally reserved as a sanctum for the Viscount's work and the Viscount's visitors. It seemed that no concession was too great for her godfather to make in the interests of getting her safely wed. Miss Harris exclaimed with outspoken pleasure as Georgiana entered: "Oh my dear! Madame Victorine has sent you the dress that she promised. It is lovely, Georgiana. Most becoming." And Viscount Benham beamed approvingly, murmuring, "Charming, a delightful picture. Quite charming. I shall never cease to be amazed at what a couple of days in town can do to alter the appearance of you ladies."

An uneasy stillness then descended upon the group as the Viscount threw obviously longing glances towards his desk and the pile of Foreign Office papers that awaited him there, and Georgiana cast longing eyes towards the windows and wondered if suicide might be the answer to all her problems.

Fortunately, before Georgiana's thoughts could become too desperate, and before the Viscount had abandoned all pretence of interest in the proceedings, Palmer announced the arrival of the Marquis of Graydon and, looking up from her corner by the window, Georgiana saw her betrothed for the first time since her fatal attempt at revenge.

She stood poised against the silk of the heavy draperies, sunlight pouring in through the windows, highlighting the dark gold of her hair. Her body was tense and erect from the strain of returning the Marquis' punctiliously correct greeting with an adequate display of calm. So preoccupied was she in absorbing the superlative formal elegance of the Marquis' appearance that she had neither time nor energy to spare for observing the impact which her own looks were creating. Overcome with a confusion of feelings that quite defined analysis, she stood silently, her head lowered, listening to the polite conversation of her betrothed, her godfather and her governess as it ebbed and flowed around her.

At last she became aware that the Marquis addressed her directly, and with a real effort she managed to face him with a tranquil face even though she was certain her knees knocked together.

"Your guardian has given us permission to spend some time together discussing the plans for our marriage, Miss Thayne. I wonder if it would be convenient for you to give me a moment or two of your time?"

Georgiana stole a quick glance at Miss Harris and the Viscount and was astonished to deduce from their happily smiling countenances that they had failed to understand the heavy sarcasm that underscored the Marquis' request. There was no point in delaying this interview any longer, however, so she replied simply, "Of course. Would you care to accompany me into the morning-room? I know my godfather is anxious to read some important despatches, and Miss Harris also mentioned to me that she had some errands which she wishes to attend to this morning."

Georgiana was miserably aware that the Marquis was regarding her with cynical eyes, and of course he knew as well as she did herself that Miss Harris had no important errands to run that morning. But she needed to talk privately with him, so she crushed her feelings of humiliation and prepared to seize the opportunity that her godfather was offering her. In view of the supposed impropriety of her behaviour hitherto, Georgiana acknowledged that Viscount Benham was being both trusting and generous in leaving her alone with the Marquis, and she made up her mind that whatever objections the Marquis raised, the ending of their betrothal must cause her godfather neither worry nor unnecessary feelings of guilt.

At this point in her reflections they arrived at the morning-room door and, bowing with exquisite and over-elaborate courtesy, the Marquis begged Georgiana to precede him into the room. The moment the door was closed, however, she felt herself crushed against the Marquis' satin waistcoat, her hands clasped within the Marquis' grasp, as he pressed a dramatic kiss upon her cheek.

"Alone at last!" he exclaimed. "Georgiana, my adored one, why did you not tell me of the tender passions you nursed for me for so *long* and so *secretly*? We could both have been spared such an anguish of desire!"

White with fury, Georgiana pulled herself out of his arms, at least part of her rage being directed at herself for finding Graydon's embrace considerably more attractive than was either proper or sensible.

"How dare you?" she said through tight lips. "You, of all people, should know that our acquaintance has been so brief and so unpleasant that no feelings of affection could possibly exist between us!"

The Marquis looked at her with cold cynicism. "I spoke of passions, Georgiana, not feelings of affection. And passion requires no time at all to come into full flower." He walked impatiently to the opposite end of the room. "I am disappointed that you failed to respond to my splendid histrionics. You gave such a lengthy and dramatic performance when last we were together, surely you cannot begrudge me a small taste of the delights of acting? And remember, you had all the additional pleasure of performing in front of an audience. We – as you cannot fail to have noticed – are quite alone. There are no witnesses to any of the lies I may care to utter."

Georgiana's fingers toyed agitatedly with one of the gold tassels that adorned the morning-room sofa. "I am well aware that I owe you an explanation of my behaviour," she said at last. "When we were with my aunt I resented being the helpless pawn in a game of your devising. How *could* I expect that you would agree to my outrageous claims and pretend that we had been secretly betrothed? Nor did I anticipate your immediate removal from Graydon Place to London. How could I see you in order to put matters right between us when you were miles away from me?"

The Marquis remained disconcertingly silent and she cried out: "Surely you cannot be surprised that I was not prepared to stand by quite tamely while my reputation and my future were bartered in that despicable fashion by you and my aunt?"

The Marquis finally spoke. "Having endured a full twenty-four hours of your company, madam, it was indeed foolish of me to anticipate your meek acquiescence in any scheme not of your own devising. My only excuse for such folly must be that I constantly confused your true personality with the character hitherto publicly associated with Miss Thayne – namely that of a simple-minded young lady, completely dominated by her aunt, docile almost to the point of childishness. I must remind you that it is *your* plan, your theatrical performance in front of Viscount Benham and Lady Elizabeth that has effectively forced me into making an offer of marriage that I would never otherwise have contemplated. Marriage – especially to acerbic, dominating females – has never been in my schemes for the immediate future."

"Oh but surely, sir, you forget one enormous advantage that I have to offer?" Georgiana refused to pay heed to the cold despair that was settling like a lump of ice somewhere in the region of her heart. "Whatever the disadvantages of my character or person, there must surely be some consolation in knowing that I possess a fortune large enough to sweeten almost any bargain. The condition of the land around Graydon has been causing you concern, I believe. Just think what can be done with the income from *my* estates!"

She stopped, silenced by the look of fury that darkened the Marquis' face.

"Despite my years in the City, madam, I have attempted to remain a gentleman," he said. "I endeavour to distinguish between my dealings of a commercial nature and my dealings with . . . friends. I beg leave to inform you that the size of your fortune was of no interest to me at the time I spoke to Viscount Benham on the subject of our marriage, and it is of no interest to me now. My financial position has changed very much from the days when I had a Marchioness to support."

Deliberately Georgiana extinguished the small flicker of hope aroused by his words. "Oh, you need not protest so vehemently, my lord," she said. "My godfather has been at pains to inform me of your generosity in the matter of our marriage settlements."

The Marquis spoke abruptly. "I had thought that in offering for your hand, Miss Thayne, I was both fulfilling my obligations as a man of honour *and* saving you from the prospect of a betrothal that you fiercely disliked. However, it now seems quite clear to me that the thought of our marriage displeases you almost as much as it displeases me. In the circumstances, it would be a little pointless for both of us to continue to sacrifice our future happiness. I realise that your godfather would not permit you to break off the engagement, but I can cry off with impunity." He spoke drily. "In a lifetime full of scandalous incidents, one more broken obligation will hardly be remarked upon."

Georgiana was shocked. "Oh no, my lord! My godfather would be very angry, and I'm afraid his influence is so great that your reputation might this time be damaged beyond all hope of repair. Remember that he is working at the centre of our government, and is not immured in the country as my aunt was at the time . . . at the time of Lady Chloë's death."

"Your concern for my reputation is touching and distinctly out of character, Miss Thayne," he responded with derision in his voice. "Can it be that you feel you have been too ready to throw away the advantages of marriage with me?"

"No," Georgiana said wildly, "I feel no regrets and no concern for you." She rubbed salt into her wounded feelings. "I had previously thought that marriage with my cousin represented the lowest point that could be reached. Now I know that there are marriages that could be worse." Stormily she whirled round to face him. "I shall rely upon you, my lord, to speak with Viscount Benham so that we may be released from an engagement that is painful to us both. Now if you would be so good as to excuse me, I would like to rejoin Lady Vaudon and Miss Harris."

The Marquis bowed in stony silence, his expression impossible to interpret, and Georgiana stalked past him, just managing to reach the sanctuary of her bedchamber before a storm of weeping overtook her. She remained stretched out on her bed, her head buried in the pillow, prey to the mournful conviction that life had now lost all hope of meaning for her, until Miss Harris' hesitant voice roused her to some effort at self-control.

She emerged from her room, red-eyed and determinedly cheerful, only to receive the message that Viscount Benham wished to see her immediately. Georgiana tried rather unsuccessfully to meet Miss Harris' gaze with a tranquillity she certainly did not feel, and came to the sad conclusion that the day's tribulations had hardly begun.

CHAPTER
TWELVE

VISCOUNT BENHAM looked searchingly at Georgiana when she entered the library, but if he noticed her red eyes and wan cheeks he decided to make no reference to them, merely nodding at her somewhat distantly and indicating that she should be seated. Georgiana perched nervously at the edge of an uncomfortable chair, and wished that her godfather might look less severe. The prospect of yet another confrontation almost left her yearning for the tranquil days of her old life at Thayne. The silence played unbearably upon her taut nerves and she burst into speech.

"You wished to talk to me, sir?"

The Viscount closed the ledger that lay open in front of him, and slowly walked round his desk to stand next to Georgiana's chair. "Graydon informs me that the winding up of his affairs in the city is proving more complex than he had anticipated, and that it would be convenient to postpone the announcement of your marriage for a week or two. He tells me that this delay is acceptable to you, if I am prepared to agree. Are you willing to postpone a formal announcement of your betrothal?"

Georgiana tried to work out why the Marquis had requested a postponement of the marriage rather than a cancellation, but her godfather was waiting for an answer and she had to speak.

"I should prefer to postpone the announcement if you please, sir," said Georgiana in a small voice. The Viscount looked unhappy, and she stumbled into an explanation.

"After all, our main reason for such haste was a fear of scandal, and it seems to me that our swift removal from Thayne has scotched the worst gossip before it ever got effectively started." She tried to inject a modicum of enthusiasm into her shaky voice. "Miss Harris and I are so enjoying the many excitements London has to offer. It is a first trip for both of us, as you know, and it seems a pity to cut it short with family parties and all the formal entertaining that accompanies the announcement of a betrothal. A delay will suit both the Marquis and myself."

Viscount Benham answered her slowly. "It is true that I have heard no gossip about your exploits with the Marquis, although you certainly do not deserve to escape so lightly from your hoydenish behaviour." He turned reproving eyes upon his godchild, and she blushed and looked suitably subdued.

"However, as it happens my return to Vienna has been delayed until July," continued Viscount Benham, "so a *short* postponement of the wedding announcements will not be of importance. But Georgiana," he spoke with renewed severity, "do not take this delay as a licence to indulge in flirtation with every young man who crosses your path. Lady Elizabeth neglected her duties in regard to your come-out, and I have excused your behaviour with the Marquis of Graydon on those grounds. But I should be failing in *my* duty as your guardian if I did not point out to you that you are not in a position to allow even a whisper of scandal to cling to your name." He looked at her almost sadly. "I am wise in the ways of the fashionable world, my dear, and whereas one piece of gossip may be conveniently ignored, two or three stories circulating about a young lady spell her social ruin."

Georgiana murmured a dutiful assent, and wondered if it was possible to feel any more wretched. The Viscount watched her expressive face for a further minute before saying quietly, "I am not a fool, my dear, whatever appearance I may have presented to you in the past. I know very well that I have not heard the full story of your relationship with the Marquis." He smiled as Georgiana turned crimson with embarrassment and astonishment.

"Despite all the evidence to the contrary, Georgiana, I believe you are a sensible girl. I am a busy man and I have learned to trust my judgment occasionally, even when the evidence appears to be against me. I merely ask that you do not give me cause for further concern on your behalf."

"Indeed, sir, I shall conduct myself with the utmost discretion." Georgiana spoke with sincere gratitude. "I cannot hope to thank you properly for the efforts you have made on my behalf. I know myself to be deeply in your debt."

"Well, well." The Viscount resumed his normal avuncular manner, patting Georgiana on the arm. "It's always a pleasure to help a pretty girl – even more agreeable if she happens to be gracing your dinner-table every night. Your husband will be a lucky man, my dear, a very lucky man."

Georgiana managed to return a weak smile and stood up to curtsy to her godfather, since he clearly considered the interview to be at an end. However lucky her husband was going to be, she reflected morosely, it did not seem that the Marquis of Graydon wished to acquire that particular piece of good fortune. She made her way back upstairs, since there were still a few minutes to wait before luncheon would be served, and thought over the interview that had just ended.

How strange that the Marquis had not requested an outright cancellation of the betrothal, but had merely asked for a delay in the public announcements! For the space of two flights of stairs Georgiana allowed herself to believe that the Marquis regretted this morning's argument as much as she did herself, and had hit upon this scheme in order to allow time for a reconciliation. This happy thought was abandoned before she reached her bedchamber, however, and she resigned herself with a cynical shrug to the realisation that the Marquis had done nothing more than seek to protect himself from recrimination at the hands of Viscount Benham. Wearily Georgiana told herself that there could be nothing simpler than to make repeated postponements of the wedding until her godfather was finally and inevitably recalled to Vienna. By utilising such tactics, the Marquis could save himself from a marriage that he dreaded and simultaneously escape the full brunt of Viscount Benham's fury.

Having successfully imputed the worst of motives to the Marquis, Georgiana sat through lunch in a mood of black despair made all the harder to bear because of the determined cheerfulness of Miss Harris and Viscount Benham. To Georgiana's distinctly jaundiced eye, even Lady Vaudon seemed to have joined the light-hearted conspiracy, and actually contributed three or four unsolicited remarks about a play she was considering seeing the following evening.

Georgiana found no difficulty at all in remaining in the depths of depression throughout the afternoon. She accompanied Miss Harris to view an exhibition of paintings at the Royal Academy, where she passed such extraordinary judgments on the portraits they examined that not even Miss Harris could hope to pretend that her pupil was paying the slightest attention to what was in front of her nose.

By the time they returned to Hanover Place, Georgiana had sufficiently recovered her good manners to apologise to Miss Harris and to mumble some entirely unconvincing excuse about a headache. Miss Harris was kind enough to accept the apology and the lie with scarcely more than a blink. Inwardly, Georgiana admitted that she longed for the opportunity to unburden herself honestly of her problems, but for a variety of reasons she hesitated to draw Miss Harris any further into her confidence.

The difficulties of her situation engaged her mind throughout dinner. Fortunately she found herself seated between two amiable young aspirants to government service who were so over-awed at being actually in Viscount Benham's house and seated next to a goddaughter of incredible beauty, that she was saved from any necessity of making intelligent conversation. It was enough merely to smile and look charming.

It was during the lengthy dinner, as she watched her hostess imperceptibly manipulating the conversation without ever appearing to do so, that Georgiana made up her mind to seek advice from Lady Vaudon. She could only hope that her chosen confidante would condescend to keep awake long enough to hear all the salient facts.

Having reached this decision some time between the

second and third courses, there were moments during the remainder of the evening when Georgiana became quite convinced that time had stopped and the painfully polite exchange of conversation would continue for ever. The two aspiring government servants beguiled the hour after dinner by mooning over Miss Thayne's enchanting air of abstraction, and Georgiana wished them heartily in Chile, or Siam, or at any other distant post that would necessitate their instant removal from Hanover Place. But at last the evening's hospitality was ended and she was at liberty to seek out her hostess.

She discovered Lady Vaudon in her dressing room, reclining on the inevitable chaise longue. She squashed a little bubble of inner laughter as she saw Lady Vaudon slip a large and heavy tome under the lace-edged pillow. Not many people, thought Georgiana, attempted to conceal the fact that they read philosophical works as a form of relaxation.

She looked blandly at Lady Vaudon and caught a slight answering gleam of humour in the plump face before the mask of indolence fell once more into place.

"I am sorry to disturb you," said Georgiana, "but I have come to ask your advice." She had considered many possible ways of broaching her problems with Lady Vaudon, and in the end had decided that only the bald truth, quickly stated, would hold Lady Vaudon's attention.

"My advice," said Lady Vaudon. "Ah."

This could hardly be considered encouragement, but Georgiana refused to be deterred. "Lady Vaudon, my betrothal to the Marquis of Graydon is not the simple matter that it seems. The circumstances of our meeting were not as we described them to my godfather, and I am very much afraid that Viscount Benham is going to find that he has been recalled to Vienna, and that I am still an unwed burden in somebody's household."

Georgiana risked a glance at Lady Vaudon. Her eyes were still open. "Naturally," continued Georgiana, "there is a grave danger that *yours* will be the hapless household selected to support me through the dangers of a budding scandal."

Lady Vaudon thought for some moments. "Perhaps you had better tell me what has really been going on between you and Graydon."

Georgiana rushed into a carefully edited account of her life with Lady Elizabeth; her betrothal to Freddie; her capture by the Marquis; her false claim of a secret betrothal; the Marquis' unexpected offer of marriage and her journey to town.

"When I saw the Marquis this morning," she concluded, "I tried to explain to him that I had pretended we were in love only as a method of escaping from Thayne Hall. Of course I had not planned to involve him *permanently* in my affairs." She looked nervously at Lady Vaudon. "You will think it reprehensible of me to have fled from my family, but I can assure you that I was imprisoned in Thayne as effectively as any of the criminals locked up in Newgate, and I had no means of resisting my aunt's determination that I should marry Frederick."

Lady Vaudon said nothing, so she plunged doggedly into the rest of her story. "The Marquis and I . . . agreed . . . this morning that it would be best if our betrothal could be terminated, and the Marquis has since spoken to my godfather. He seems to have asked Viscount Benham for a postponement of the formal announcements. I don't know what I should do next, Lady Vaudon."

"You wish me to speak for you to my brother?" asked Lady Vaudon. "You wish me to make it plain to him that the betrothal is over – that, in essence, it has never been?"

Her guest flushed an extremely deep shade of crimson. Her fingers twisted nervously among the blue ribbons of her gown. "That was not precisely what I had in mind," said Georgiana.

"Ah," said Lady Vaudon. "You are, perhaps, embarrassed by the false position in which you find yourself. You wish to alert me – since I am your hostess and also your chaperone – to the fact that you will require a guardian after your godfather returns to Vienna?"

Georgiana looked distracted. The expensive blue ribbons were well on the way to being ruined. "I do not wish to impose myself upon you," said Georgiana, "but that is not precisely the problem that troubles me."

"Well," said Lady Vaudon, "you wish to tell me, perhaps, that you have been foolish enough to fall in love with Graydon, and even more foolishly have contrived to send him packing. And now you wish to ask me how you should get him back?"

"Yes," said Georgiana, "I think that is the problem I wished to discuss with you."

"Your taste in men," returned Lady Vaudon, "is better than your taste in clothes."

Georgiana allowed herself to be diverted. "Do you know the Marquis?" she asked with interest.

"We used to know each other rather well. He was quite good company until that dreadful woman got her hooks into him."

"Lady Chloë? You considered her dreadful?"

"She was a vicious woman with fewer morals than an alley cat," said Lady Vaudon with supreme disregard for conventional decorum. "I've no doubt she'd taken her first lover before Graydon got her home from the bridal trip. He can only be grateful she didn't start breeding, for he would never have known whose child he was being asked to father."

"Were you acquainted with the Marquis at the time of his wife's . . . when Lady Chloë . . . that is to say . . ." Georgiana looked up and caught Lady Vaudon's sardonic gaze. She drew a deep breath and said bluntly, "My aunt, Lady Elizabeth, has always maintained that the Marquis of Graydon was responsible for the death of Lady Chloë. Are you aware of this story?"

"My good girl, all of London was aware of the story because your aunt made it her business to spread rumours and Graydon made no effort to stop her. He was always ridiculously puffed up in his notions of honour. You should know that – look what a mess it's got you into." Lady Vaudon lapsed into a contemplative silence, and Georgiana was forced to prod her into further speech.

"Do *you* believe that the Marquis of Graydon shot Lady Chloë?"

"Of course not," snapped Lady Vaudon. "Chloë had taken young de Vigny as her lover, and the story was all over town. It was particularly galling for Graydon, because de Vigny was his cousin and hardly more than a boy. He had given up all pretence of living with his wife by this time, but the scandal became so fierce that he was forced to post down to Graydon Place and make an effort to quieten things down – for de Vigny's sake as much as for his own." Lady Vaudon shrugged a world-weary shoulder. "I heard a rumour that de Vigny attempted suicide and that Lady Chloë was killed when the Marquis struggled to get the gun away from his cousin."

Georgiana was unable to repress a slight shudder of horror as she visualised the scene, and Lady Vaudon said sharply, "Not a very edifying story, but then Lady Chloë dragged everybody down to her own low level."

"It seems there is considerable justification for the Marquis' bitterness towards my aunt," said Georgiana.

Lady Vaudon made no effort to respond to so obvious a remark, and leaned back against the pillows giving every indication of losing interest in such ancient problems. Hastily Georgiana recalled her attention to the other, more current, matters waiting for solution.

"If I am not be be left a permanent spinster on your hands, Lady Vaudon, there is still the question of my betrothal to the Marquis to be considered. At the moment, it does not look very likely to result in a marriage."

Lady Vaudon regarded Georgiana with irritation. "You are young, single, rich, attractive, and – since you came to me – well dressed. I was relatively poor, plain, and cursed with more brains than most girls could dream about in their worst nightmares. If I could manage to find two perfectly acceptable husbands, I cannot see why you anticipate any difficulty in bringing Graydon to heel."

Georgiana failed to find encouragement. "But Lady Vaudon, I have no experience with men. I have spent all my life in a quiet village. The squire is sixty-two years old, and the vicar ranks all women slightly lower than dogs and several degrees lower than horses. It is a little difficult for me to see precisely how I am to . . . er . . . bring the Marquis to heel."

"Besides," she added wistfully, "it would be so much pleasanter if he should choose to come to me willingly."

Lady Vaudon grunted. "I can see I shall have to escort you to some parties," she observed. "Believe me, after one week you will have all the unattached men in town flocking to your side. I need only whisper the size of your fortune into two or three of the proper ears, and Benham will be sweeping the aspirants to your hand from the front door." She looked at Georgiana meditatively. "With your looks, it's even possible that some of the suitors will really wish to marry you rather than your fortune."

Georgiana looked bewildered, then self-conscious. "But you see, it is Graydon whom I wish to marry, even if some of these other suitors are sincere."

Lady Vaudon looked discouraged. "Georgiana, I am trying to help, but you are making things very difficult for me. Of *course* I do not expect you to fall in love with any of these mythical suitors! I merely wish you to be attentive to them whenever your Marquis is there to observe you. And I," said Lady Vaudon with evident satisfaction, "will see to it that he is *frequently* there."

Georgiana experienced an insensible lightening of her spirits, and she smiled more happily than had seemed possible a few minutes before. "I have no confidence in my own abilities, Lady Vaudon. But if you are at work behind the scenes, the Marquis and I will undoubtedly be married before the month is out. It seems I am never going to be able to thank you or my godfather suffiently."

Lady Vaudon looked gratified. "It was boring here before you came," she said, and closed her eyes.

CHAPTER
THIRTEEN

An invitation to dine with Lady Vaudon or with her brother Viscount Benham was an honour much sought after by every aspirant to government service, and by many who desired nothing more concrete than social acclaim. Thus, although neither Viscount Benham nor his sister had recently participated in the more frivolous activities of the London season, Georgiana rapidly discovered that the Benham name was a miraculous passport to the heights of social success.

She and Miss Harris found themselves caught up in a whirl of frenetic activity, brought about partly by Lady Vaudon's efforts and partly by Viscount Benham's sudden determination to make his godchild known to all the distant relatives, old friends and persons of general consequence that she should have met at the time of her emergence from the schoolroom.

At the end of a week of lunches, dinners, musical afternoons and picnics by the river, Lady Vaudon was able to announce her protégée with quiet pride, "You are a Success." Georgiana accepted the truth of this statement, without deriving very much pleasure from it. She knew that the advantages of her strikingly beautiful appearance would, in normal circumstances, have been offset by the all too evident intelligence which she no longer troubled to conceal. However, Lady Vaudon's artful hints concerning the huge Thayne fortune invariably preceded her introduction into a new set of people, and Georgiana never lacked for assiduous and avowedly devoted courtiers.

Some of the young men were possibly even sincere in their protestations of admiration, but since Georgiana listened to their conversation with considerably less than half her attention – the other half was invariably devoted either to observing the Marquis or wondering where he might be – she was never able to distinguish the genuine admirers from the fortune-hunters. She solved the problem by despising them all, and spent her spare moments chastising herself for imagining that the Marquis had any less interest in her fortune than the rest of her suitors.

The Marquis, whether at Lady Vaudon's instigation or simply because of coincidence, was present at the majority of functions attended by Georgiana and Miss Harris. On the first few occasions that they met, the Marquis greeted Georgiana with a punctilious courtesy that immediately drove her into an exasperated flirtation with whichever of her aspiring suitors happened to be closest at hand. After three uncomfortable evening parties, Georgiana's efforts to arouse the Marquis' jealousy were rewarded by seeing him arrive at Lady Selling's rout-party in the company of an entrancingly beautiful and raven-haired widow, whose vivacity of manner was outdone only by the transparency of her attire. Georgiana, trying hard to ignore the sparkle of interest in the Marquis' eyes whenever they happened to light upon the highly visible charms of this luscious widow, responded so favourably to the tentative advances of the young man sitting beside her, that he instantly decided to test his fortune the following morning and make her a declaration in form. He was disillusioned to find that she seemed to experience difficulty in recalling his name when he presented himself in Hanover Place early on Wednesday morning, and left without declaring himself, bitterly forswearing female company for ever.

It was after this incident that Georgiana made her way to Lady Vaudon's boudoir and placed herself firmly in the doorway. "It is of no use, Lady Vaudon," she said. "It is quite plain that the Marquis has . . . other interests. There is no point in forcing yourself into needless activity. We may as well accustom ourselves to the thought that I shall be a burden upon you for many years to come."

Lady Vaudon answered languidly. "Oh come, my dear Georgiana! If you have decided to give up all thoughts of the Marquis, Benham has already received a number of perfectly suitable requests from young men of good family and tolerable means who wish to pay their addresses. Simply select your favourite from among them and have done with the matter."

Georgiana looked cross. "You know that I do not wish to marry any of these suitable young men of good family."

"Well then," said Lady Vaudon, "I suggest you wait until after the ball I am giving next week before lapsing into a state of total decline."

Georgiana persisted in looking dejected. "How is one more party supposed to change his deeply-rooted indifference?"

Lady Vaudon spoke slowly and patiently, as to a child. "I have seen no evidence that the Marquis is indifferent to your behaviour. On the contrary. And as far as my brother is concerned, Graydon is still your betrothed, even if the engagement is not announced.

He will naturally be invited to the family dinner that precedes the ball, and he will also be constrained to dance with you. Since the Marquis is not blind, he cannot have failed to observe that you are a beautiful and desirable woman. He is already unable to remain in a ballroom with you without watching every partner you take and every smile you bestow. Surely you can manage to convince him that marriage offers compensations for the sacrifice of bachelor freedom?"

Lady Vaudon looked thoroughly exasperated. "You could tell him, perhaps, that not all women are like Lady Chloë, and that six years is quite long enough to run away from a memory."

Georgiana refused to be comforted. "You know full well that I could not possibly suggest any such thing to him." With supreme irrelevance she added, "He never looks at me as he looked at that . . . at that . . . at Mrs. Beecham."

"And that is very fortunate for us all," said Lady Vaudon testily, "or he would find himself excluded from all the respectable drawing-rooms. Mrs. Beecham is a widow, already twice married, and barely tolerated on the fringes of society. Her behaviour, and the behaviour of her escort towards her, will necessarily be different from that expected of a man escorting a young girl who has yet to make her official debut. Now, Georgiana, the situation is already quite difficult enough. Please do not be for ever adding imaginary complications. I can assure you that the Marquis of Graydon has no intention of marrying Mrs. Beecham, and any other relationship he may have had with her is of no possible interest to you."

Lady Vaudon collapsed against the pillows of her chaise-longue, and Georgiana was left with the doubtful consolation of picturing Mrs. Beecham and the Marquis of Graydon locked together in a passionate embrace, unhindered by the fetters of matrimony. The pangs of jealousy that she suffered quite overcame the small measure of consolation, but pride came to her rescue – at least on public occasions – and she reserved a specially warm and insincere smile for the Marquis and Mrs. Beecham when next she encountered them.

In an effort to assuage her aching feelings, she threw herself into the activities remaining before Lady Vaudon's ball with a hectic enthusiasm that threatened to exhaust even her robust constitution. Her brittle effervescence marked her as the newest and most interesting star on London's social horizon, and Georgiana danced away the nights with an endless supply of brilliant smiles and a painfully heavy heart.

Lady Elizabeth arrived in town on a particularly fine Thursday afternoon. The journey from Thayne had been uneventful, and she stepped out of the family carriage to be greeted by cloudless skies, warm sunshine, and a gentle westerly breeze that hinted of approaching summer. Her mood as she crossed the threshold of Thayne House was ambivalent, but she had not spent many hours listening to her husband and son before her spirits were enveloped in a black rage that mixed ill with the spring sunshine.

Lady Elizabeth had once been a young girl with plentiful intelligence, reasonable education, moderate looks and no fortune, who felt herself obliged to accept the marriage offered by William Thayne – at that time merely a younger brother to the third baron, with few expectations of ever inheriting the title. Half a lifetime of subduing her superior mind to the inferior judgments of her husband, and of economising in order to pay for the debts incurred by his compulsive gambling, had resulted in a bitterness of spirit that inevitably required an outlet.

For the last six years, the attractions of her role as lady of the manor had sufficed to fill the void left by an unsatisfactory marriage. The social power that she wielded in the country – as evidenced by the successful ostracism of the Marquis of Graydon – was a balm that had soothed and comforted her for the inadequacies of her husband and her son. Her manipulation of Georgiana's destiny, and the prospect of acquiring her niece's fortune for Frederick, had been an added solace.

Now, in the space of a few short weeks, the life that she had so carefully built up around herself lay crumbling at her feet. Viscount Benham's return from Vienna had set in motion a series of events that left her once more alone, her position of authority – and even her recent financial security – all threatened. And at the centre of these unpleasant changes loomed the figure of the transformed Georgiana. Unable to fault the Viscount, and unwilling to apportion blame to her only child, Lady Elizabeth poured the distilled fury of a circumscribed lifetime on to Georgiana's unsuspecting head.

It was bad enough when she first arrived at Thayne House and had to endure the constant repinings of Freddie, who was by now feeling thoroughly aggrieved that the ravishing Georgiana had been snatched from his grasp. But it became unendurable when Lady Elizabeth found herself forced to listen with apparent gratification as old acquaintances congratulated her upon Georgiana's meteoric progress across the London scene.

Even this discomfiture was as nothing to the silent rage that consumed her at Lady Vaudon's ball. Invitation cards for the family dinner that preceded the ball had naturally been sent to Frederick, and to Lord and Lady Thayne. When Georgiana entered the reception room, Lady Elizabeth found herself swamped by a painful emotion that she failed to identify as overmastering jealousy.

Never in her wildest dreams had Lady Elizabeth expected to see her niece shimmering on the threshold of a ballroom, every line of her perfect body revealed by a gown of clinging blue crepe. Sapphires glowed darkly against the white of Georgiana's neck, pale rosebuds wreathed the shining gold of her hair, a combination of artless innocence and sophistication that was startling in its effects. Lady Elizabeth was furious to see Freddie reduced to goggle-eyed wonderment, and she observed acridly that none of the men present remained entirely unaffected.

It would have seemed that Lady Elizabeth's cup of bitterness must be full, but the vexations of the evening had hardly begun. Shaken out of her normal icy control, Lady Elizabeth could not refrain from taunting Georgiana in a voice loaded with accumulated animosity, but far from shattering Georgiana's new composure, these tactics merely served to stir the Marquis of Graydon into a languid, but determined, defence of his betrothed. Lady Elizabeth had the bitter satisfaction of observing the shy smiles of gratitude that flashed from her niece to the Marquis, and assimilated the even more unpalatable knowledge that these smiles were reciprocated with a lazy grace belied by the hidden passion that warmed the Marquis' gaze whenever it turned to Georgiana.

She awoke on the morning after the ball to find her emotions once more under cold control and her mind functioning with its habitual ruthless efficiency. She breakfasted impatiently, dressed quickly, and sent for her son.

Freddie entered her dressing room with evident apprehension, and greeted his mother warily. She waited restlessly for him to be seated and then said abruptly: "Do you still want to marry Georgie?"

Freddie looked harassed, but could not prevent a certain note of eagerness from creeping into his voice.

"Why yes, Mamma," he said. "But she is engaged to Graydon."

Lady Elizabeth shrugged. "There has been no official announcement of the suit. Viscount Benham took it upon himself to interfere unnecessarily in our plans, and I have decided that there is no reason for you to lose Georgie if you would care to have her."

Freddie's voice revealed his uneasiness. "Do you wish me to propose to Georgie again, Mamma? I don't think Viscount Benham would care for me to do that. Besides," he added with unexpected honesty, "I don't suppose Georgie would have me. You only had to look at her dancing with Graydon last night to know she's head-over-heels in love with him."

"Nonsense," Lady Elizabeth said firmly. "Georgiana is like any other young girl and responds to a masterful hand upon the reins. If you wish to have Georgie for a wife you will have to take the initiative. Once you and your cousin are safely wed, we have merely to present Viscount Benham with the *fait accompli*. We are only taking a leaf out of Graydon's own book, after all."

"But how am I to marry Georgie when I may not even

see her privately to pay my addresses?" asked Freddie in bewilderment.

Lady Elizabeth sighed and took a tight hold on her irritation. "You will not, of course, be able to make Georgiana a declaration in form. However, Lady Vaudon plans to escort Georgiana to a ridotto at Vauxhall Gardens tonight. I am to be one of the party. You were invited but I shall make your excuses. At the appropriate moment I shall contrive to escort Georgiana to the carriageway at the north edge of the gardens where you will be waiting. Simply drive Georgiana to Redlands Manor and keep her hidden until we are able to make arrangements for someone to marry you. The Vicar of Thayne will doubtless oblige us, if I procure a special licence."

Freddie considered the idea with a breathless mixture of fear and excitement. He pictured Georgie, the entrancing new Georgie, captive by his side and forced to take him seriously as a man to be reckoned with. It was a heady prospect, but caution prevailed.

"You are forgetting about Graydon," he warned glumly. "Once he knows that I've taken Georgie he will follow us and challenge me to a duel. You cannot expect me to face up to the Marquis, not even for Georgie."

"No," said Lady Elizabeth "I could certainly not expect you to face up to the Marquis." She sighed. "Don't worry. Redlands Manor has always been part of your father's personal estate, so although it is quite close to Thayne I doubt very much if Viscount Benham has ever heard of it. Besides, I shall leave a note in Georgiana's handwriting, confessing to her guardian that she has eloped. If I deliberately fail to mention the name of her supposed lover, there will be no reason for Benham or for Graydon to suspect our role in this.

Lord knows, Georgiana now has a sufficient number of admirers to make it almost impossible to identify her favourites!"

Freddie offered further protests, but Lady Elizabeth easily calmed his fears since he was willing to be convinced. Visions of Georgiana danced entrancingly before his eyes, supporting him through the trials of organising a carriage and swift horses, selecting servants to accompany him, and providing the clothing he considered necessary to his comfort. He could hardly wait for evening to fall, and bade an incoherent farewell to his mother as she set off for Hanover Place.

Georgiana ate frugally of the shaved ham and sipped the mulled red wine that was part of the traditional fare of Vauxhall Gardens. A coloratura soprano had just finished her bravura performance of baroque arias, and Georgiana was pleased to be free to devote her attention to the constant passage of visitors making their way past Lady Vaudon's box.

After the heady delights of yesterday evening she found it an effort to pretend any interest in the colourful scene around her, but Lady Vaudon had assured her that no stay in London was complete without a visit to the gardens, and the other members of Lady Vaudon's party were giving every evidence of entire satisfaction with their situation. Even Lady Elizabeth had unbent a little and seemed by the friendliness of her remarks to be making a silent apology for the harshness of her behaviour the day before.

Ruefully, Georgiana accepted that her lack of pleasure stemmed not from any failings in the entertainment provided for her delectation, but rather from the absence of the Marquis of Graydon, who had declined his invitation – albeit with obvious regret. He had smiled at Georgiana as they ate supper together at Lady Vaudon's ball and said, "I wish I could be with you, but I really do have affairs to be settled in the City. Tomorrow night promises to be the last dinner I shall have with my former partner. Mr. Jessop was very good to me at a time when I felt myself to be at odds with the world. I cannot cancel this final evening together just because I had far rather be elsewhere and in other company."

A reminiscent smile touched Georgiana's lips and her eyes softened as she re-lived the pleasures of waltzing in the Marquis' firm and possessive arms. No precise mention had been made of the betrothal that still hovered between them, but Georgiana felt confident that it needed only a drive in the park, or some other opportunity of private conversation, for all misunderstandings to be resolved between them.

A general jostling at the table warned her of the exodus about to take place, and indeed the box was soon emptied of all its occupants save Lady Vaudon, who waved aside suggestions that she should come and admire the fireworks just now being let off. Georgiana would have been more than willing to keep Lady Vaudon company, but Lady Elizabeth took her arm with a friendly smile and remarked, "You should not deprive yourself of this opportunity to see one of London's most famous sights. Lady Vaudon will be quite comfortable with her maid and the footman to attend to her needs."

Pleased that her aunt seemed at last to have forgiven her, Georgiana allowed herself to be drawn in the direction of the artificial lake which served as a background to the firework display. The rest of their party – Miss Harris, two of Lady Vaudon's young cousins, and a

Lieutenant in the Hussars whose relationship to the Benham household Georgiana had not yet quite fathomed — were soon lost to view as they hurried through the throng of spectators now pressing round Georgiana and Lady Elizabeth.

The May night was clear and warm, ideal for an exhibition of elaborate pyrotechnics, and Georgiana felt herself caught up in the enchantment of the complex and often beautiful displays. She was aware of the mass of bodies all around her, but failed to find this oppressive. She was therefore surprised and alarmed when she felt Lady Elizabeth sway against her side, and quickly supported her before she could faint quite away.

"Quickly, Georgiana. Please help me to get some air . . . I feel . . . I feel . . . overcome."

Georgiana was nonplussed at this sign of physical weakness in a woman she had always thought of as virtually indomitable in mind and body. Lady Elizabeth's face did appear flushed and strangely mottled, beads of sweat standing out on her brow. With murmured apologies, Georgiana forced a way through the crowd and escorted her aunt to the edge of the meadow. She was relieved to discover that her aunt could walk quite capably, since the men of the party were all still invisible.

Lady Elizabeth sank down upon a rustic bench and fanned herself with a hand that trembled. "You must forgive me, my dear, for depriving you of your entertainment. I should never have come tonight, but I did not wish to give the appearance of . . ." Her voice trailed into a pathetically weak silence. "My carriage is waiting for me at the north entrance to the gardens. Would you offer me your arm as far as my coach — I really do not feel capable of staying at this ridotto any longer."

Georgiana offered her aunt her own handkerchief, freshly sprinkled with lavender water from her reticule. "Of course I will escort you, Aunt Elizabeth, if you wish it. But would it not be better for me to call for assistance and send one of the servants to bring your carriage nearer to the main part of the gardens? It will be a long walk to the northern entrance."

Lady Elizabeth managed a wan smile. "I do not wish to break up the party by making this foolish indisposition public knowledge. My maid and two footmen are waiting with the carriage, so I shall be well able to spare you an escort back to Lady Vaudon's box."

Georgiana felt there was some reason to agree that Lady Elizabeth's illness would break up the evening if it became known, and although she would not personally have been distressed to return home, Lady Vaudon's other guests would probably be glad to see the end of the firework display. She and Lady Elizabeth therefore walked at a leisurely pace across the grounds of Vauxhall which, although never quite deserted, were considerably less populated in this area of quiet wooded walks.

They finally reached the carriage lane, and found several chatting groups of servants waiting the return of their masters. Georgiana could not at first spot the Thayne family crest, and while her eyes were straining to see the familiar carriage, her astonished gaze alighted upon Freddie, who was standing beside a smart travelling chaise drawn by four horses.

"Why, Aunt Elizabeth, there is Freddie. Was he expecting to meet you here?" she asked.

Lady Elizabeth was suddenly overcome by a fresh spasm, and Georgiana, relieved that her cousin was providentially available to assist her with this sudden and mysterious ailment, called out, "Freddie! Freddie! Over here. Come quickly."

Freddie cast an anxious look at the lolling groups of coachmen, and ran over to his mother. "Good lord, Georgie!" he remarked. "No need to let all the world know my name."

"Your mother is not well, Freddie, and we need your assistance to escort her home." She gave another look round the waiting coaches. "I cannot see the family carriage," she said, "although my aunt said that it would be here. Never mind. It is a godsend that you chanced to wait in this particular spot."

Freddie's worried glance slid over his mother's flushed face. He was perplexed by the effectiveness of her acting, and wondered for a dreadful moment if she was actually suffering a genuine spasm. Her impatient voice cut through his indecision.

"Support my right arm, Freddie. Georgiana will remain at my left hand."

They stumbled over to the carriage, when to Georgiana's consternation she felt her arm seized in a vice-like grasp, and heard Lady Elizabeth's voice, returned to its naturally commanding timbre, ordering Freddie to lift her into the carriage. Before Georgiana had time to do more than utter a brief cry, she was hoisted into the interior of the coach and Freddie, with an unusual show of agility, had sprung in beside her slamming the door shut as soon as he had shouted out instructions to the coachman.

"Freddie!" cried Georgiana. "Are you gone quite mad? What are you doing? Your mother . . . Lady Vaudon . . ."

Freddie smiled smugly. "It was a good plot, wasn't it?" he said comfortably. "The Marquis of Graydon persuaded you to run off with him to be married even though you were supposed to be betrothed to me. Well, now I have run off with you and you shall marry me, even though you are supposed to be engaged to the Marquis." He sighed with satisfaction at this splendid piece of retribution.

"Don't be ridiculous, Freddie," Georgiana said. "You know that Viscount Benham wishes me to marry the Marquis of Graydon, and he will be seriously displeased when he discovers what has happened."

"Oh, mamma has seen to all that," Freddie answered airily. "She's left a note for Benham telling him that you've eloped."

"Freddie!" Georgiana's voice shook slightly. "You know very well that I don't wish to marry you, and that *really* you do not wish to marry me. You have allowed your mamma to overcome your own judgment."

"Oh, no!" said Freddie. "I like you now that you are so thin and pretty. And when we are married we shall be able to do just as we please and neither my mother nor my father will be able to stop us, because I shall have all your fortune."

Georgiana looked at Freddie in silent despair. She hoped fervently that her godfather, prompted by Lady Vaudon, would be suspicious of the elopement note and suspect that his godchild had not left of her own free will. The reassuring thought crossed her mind that no vicar, however secularly minded, would be prepared to marry her to Freddie if she once protested that the marriage was against her wishes. However, it could well be days before she was actually traced and Viscount Benham might yet be faced with the difficult task of deciding which of her abductors had compromised her more.

An irresponsible giggle bubbled to Georgiana's lips. There was a certain intoxicating satisfaction to be derived from compromising oneself with two different suitors within the space of a month – and entirely without co-operation on her part.

The horses had been given their heads and the carriage plunged swiftly through the night. Georgiana sighed and rested her head against the corner squabs. After two kidnappings, she mused, she was becoming adept at adjusting herself to the rigours of captivity. The swaying motion of the coach rocked her tired body in an insidious lullaby, and she fell asleep thinking that since she had outwitted the Marquis of Graydon, there was no reason to suppose that Poor Cousin Freddie would be able to keep her captive for very long.

CHAPTER
FOURTEEN

LADY VAUDON relaxed against the comfortable cushions of the box and allowed a placid wave of well-being to wash over her. Georgiana looked like being happily settled after a nerve-trying two weeks, her guests were at a comfortable distance and presumably enjoying themselves, and she was at liberty to contemplate the passing scene without any necessity for personal involvement.

The satisfactions of her situation were unceremoniously cut short, however, by the sudden and unexpected arrival of her brother, who strode up to the box giving every appearance of a man who is at the end of his tether. Lady Vaudon made a mental grimace, but appeared outwardly much as ever. She raised her hand and murmured, "Benham! How good of you to join us."

Viscount Benham looked at her crossly. "You know very well, Adelaide, that I had not the slightest intention of coming here tonight. And as your agile mind has undoubtedly already concluded, I have been forced here upon a matter of some urgency. Where is Georgiana?"

A brief flicker of alarm crossed Lady Vaudon's features, but she said as passively as ever, "Why she has gone to view the firework display; she and Lady Elizabeth left here together." She added curtly, "Why do you want her?"

Viscount Benham thrust a piece of paper into his sister's hands. "If you read that, ma'am, you will understand my need to find Georgiana. Are you *quite* sure that she is still with the others?"

Lady Vaudon lifted her head from the letter for a moment. "Benham, I am seated – as you can see – alone in our box. The fireworks, which Georgiana is supposed to be viewing, are being exploded over by the lake. I can no more be sure of your god-daughter's precise whereabouts than you. However," she turned her attention once again to the letter and finished reading it. "However," she repeated, "I would lay odds that Georgiana was planning no sudden flight when she left my side this evening, whatever this letter may say."

"I am well aware, ma'am, that you have taken one of your inexplicable likings to the wretched girl, and indeed I have found myself beguiled . . ." He broke off in some exasperation. "Oh lord, here comes that dreadful Thayne creature. What am I going to say to *her*!"

Lady Vaudon observed Lady Elizabeth's agitated progress along the walk. "I would think," she answered drily, "that you will not need to say anything to Lady Elizabeth. She gives every appearance of wishing to say a great deal to *you*."

At this moment a panting and seeingly distraught Lady Elizabeth arrived at the door to the box. She caught sight of Viscount Benham and emitted a groan of distress.

"Viscount Benham! Oh, my lord, thank God you are here. It's Georgiana!" She paused dramatically and drew a shuddering breath. "I blame myself! It was so crowded down by the lake that I fear I did not pay the attention that I ought! One minute she was by my side, and the next minute she was gone. I struggled to find a path out through the crowd, and I am sure I saw her in the distance. But she was with . . . there was a man with her . . . They ignored me and just hurried away into a waiting carriage." She threw a handkerchief over her face and gave way to the sobs that wracked her. "What are we to do? She will bring scandal on us all!"

Viscount Benham looked furious. "You see, Adelaide? Your optimism was unfounded. I should have known better than to suppose her behaviour with the Marquis of Graydon was an isolated incident. She is clearly utterly lacking in moral sense, and I have a good mind simply to wash my hands of the whole affair and leave her to reap the consequences of her own misconduct."

"Have you quite finished?" asked Lady Vaudon quietly. "Or are we planning to bring this particular episode of family history to the attention of the entire *beau monde*?"

Viscount Benham acknowledged that it would be more appropriate to continue the discussion inside the box, and he escorted a tottering Lady Elizabeth round to the entrance. The footman opened the door, bowed silently and withdrew to a dark corner, just as if he had no interest at all in the exciting carryings-on.

Lady Elizabeth flopped into a chair, and Lady Vaudon said with deceptive mildness, "It is unlike you, my dear Lady Elizabeth, to allow yourself to be overset. I had not realised that your affection for Georgiana was so strong."

"It's not," Lady Elizabeth snapped curtly. "My concern is for the family honour."

"Oh, surely there is no need to distress yourself so severely, my dear? After all, the Thayne family honour has survived several years of gambling and wenching by your husband and your son. Surely we can expect it similarly to survive any minor faults in your niece's behaviour?"

"I do not consider an elopement a minor fault," returned Lady Elizabeth tartly.

"Well, never mind that now," said Viscount Benham, relieved to see Lady Elizabeth so much recovered. "Our task is to decide what must be done next."

The return of the other guests delayed further conversation while introductions were made to Viscount Benham. Lady Vaudon had the happy idea of using his presence as an excuse for a hasty return to Hanover Place. She muttered something vague about government despatches, made no effort to suggest why these should require *her* withdrawal from Vauxhall, and sent the Hussar lieutenant and the young cousins so swiftly on their way that they were returned to their lodgings before they recalled to mind the absence of Miss Georgiana Thayne from the cluster of people in the box.

Miss Harris, Lady Elizabeth, and Viscount Benham completed the return journey to Hanover Place in a mire of indecisive discussion. Viscount Benham, so confident in his diplomatic judgments, veered alternatively between condemning Georgiana out of hand, offering her one last chance at reform and – prompted by Miss Harris – clutching at the fragile hope that there was some misunderstanding and that Georgiana had not, in fact, eloped. On this last alternative, Lady Elizabeth would allow no reliance to be placed. She, of them all, knew Georgiana best, and it had been clear to her that Georgiana was accompanying her unknown escort quite willingly and happily. Lady Vaudon remained silent.

Upon arrival in Hanover Place, Viscount Benham retired immediately to his study, taking with him a distraught Miss Harris and a now-recovered Lady Elizabeth. It was only after their discussion had continued without resolution for almost an hour that Miss Harris remarked,

"I know Lady Vaudon is easily fatigued, but perhaps we might intrude upon her rest on this occasion. It is, after all, somewhat of an emergency."

Viscount Benham noticed for the first time that his sister was not present, and wiser in the ways of Lady Vaudon than either of the other two, he said, "Oh lord. What's she up to now?" He rang for the butler and sent an impatient message requesting his sister's presence in the library. An impassive Palmer returned very shortly carrying a sheet of crested paper that bore a simple message, "I am busy. I will talk to you later."

Viscount Benham crumpled the sheet of paper in his fist and did not reveal its contents to the two ladies. Instead he bowed to them politely and said that Lady Vaudon wished to speak with him privately. He courteously made arrangements for Lady Elizabeth's escort home, and urged Miss Harris to get some rest.

"Do not worry," he said to them both, "I shall certainly see that you are appraised of any news that we have as soon as it is forthcoming." Both ladies received his reassurances with wan smiles: Miss Harris because she feared for Georgiana's safety, and Lady Elizabeth because she suspected that Lady Vaudon offered a threat to her plans. Viscount Benham just managed to curb his patience long enough to see them out of his study without screaming.

He entered his sister's dressing-room without ceremony, and stood rooted to the spot when he discovered her still formally dressed in her velvet evening gown, talking to the Marquis of Graydon who was spurred and booted in readiness for a hard ride. Viscount Benham greeted him briefly, and with difficulty stifled all of the several reproaches that he wished to hurl at his sister's head.

Lady Vaudon looked at him with amusement. "Sit down, Benham. You too, Graydon, if you wish." She smiled. "The Marquis has just this moment responded to my message, Benham. I suggested that he should join us here prepared for a long, fast ride."

Viscount Benham said stiffly, "I cannot imagine that this affair will be of any concern to Graydon. Whatever interest he might have had in Georgiana must inevitably be cancelled by this latest escapade of hers. Good God! No gentleman could be expected to accept Georgiana after reading a letter such as she wrote to me!"

The Marquis of Graydon looked first bewildered and then annoyed. "You might be good enough to explain to me what this is all about," he said coldly.

Lady Vaudon forestalled her brother's efforts at explanation. "Georgiana went missing this evening when she was in the charge of Lady Elizabeth. My brother, who did not accompany us to Vauxhall, has meanwhile discovered a letter from Georgiana that you may care to read."

The Marquis seized the letter that Lady Vaudon offered him and cast incredulous eyes over the contents. He went white and handed the missive back to Lady Vaudon with a curt bow.

"I shall be happy to assist in tracing Miss Thayne. You will realise that I could not possibly marry her?" He looked at Lady Vaudon's cynical expression and added, "Not for the reasons you are imagining, madam, but simply because I could not contemplate another marriage with an unwilling bride. I have already endured one marriage that was brought about against the express wishes of the lady in question. I shall never again make that mistake."

Viscount Benham coughed. "No need for you to have been brought into the matter at this stage. I wish m'sister had waited until things were clearer before she approached you. I quite understand *your* position. What I don't understand is what Georgiana is up to. Nobody told her she had to marry you – quite the opposite. She was crazy for you, and we were all trying to tell her she should have her cousin. If she didn't want you in the first place, why did she kick up such a fuss in order to get you? Ah, women!" He sighed profoundly. "There's no understanding them."

"On the contrary," replied the Marquis harshly, "the matter is all too easy to explain. While Miss Thayne was confined to the narrow boundaries of her home, I have no doubt that I presented a relatively eligible prospect. Now that her horizons have been widened and her success with the *ton* assured, she naturally no longer wishes to tie herself to such a doubtful bridegroom as myself. The disadvantages of the match must now be obvious to her."

Lady Vaudon looked more angry than her brother could previously remember. "What nonsense is this?" she asked irascibly. "I have frequently observed the extraordinary inability of gentlemen to pursue even the most simple logic in dealing with their womenfolk, but I should have thought that you, Graydon, would by now have acquired a suffcently wide experience to know when a woman is madly in love with you."

Lady Vaudon paused and drew an irritable breath. "Even if she had not chosen to confide in me, *I* would have seen that Georgiana is eating her heart out over you, and has been ever since you so foolishly took her protestations at face value and released her from her engagement. *I* know very well that she would be hard put to identify any one of the young flibbertigibbets that flock around her looking for a share in that entrancing Thayne fortune. *I* know that she spends every evening looking for your arrival, and that if you don't turn up *I* know that she considers the evening as utterly lost. Where have you been looking that you have not seen this as well? Too busy flirting with that repellingly vulgar Mrs. Beecham, I suppose?"

"Mrs. Beecham is the merest acquaintance," the Marquis returned stiffly. "Miss Thayne made it clear to me that she found my company tedious. I therefore sought relaxation with a woman not likely to make demands either on my time or my emotions."

"Oh, stuff!" said Lady Vaudon inelegantly. "I have never known two people contrive to make such a mull of their affairs. You are both so stiff-necked and high-falutin' that Benham had better get you married to one another as quick as may be. You are obviously ideally suited."

"You are forgetting, madam," said the Marquis in slightly thawed accents, "that Georgiana has chosen to flee. I cannot believe that this indicates any particular depth of affection for myself." He smiled somewhat ruefully. "I confess that I should be happy to believe that your estimate of Georgiana's feelings was correct."

"And *I* confess that I have found myself very much attracted to Georgiana while she has been staying with us," said Viscount Benham. "In many ways she reminds me of her mother, who was a delightful person, although unfortunately rather serious-minded for a female. But my dear," he turned apologetically to his sister, "it is rather difficult to dispute the evidence we have before us. I think we have only to consider whether we should attempt one further rescue, or whether we must – with regret – leave Georgiana to face the severe penalties of her reckless behaviour."

Lady Vaudon sighed. "I have just explained to you that Georgiana *could not* have chosen to elope. Therefore we have to consider the true significance of this 'evidence' you believe to be indisputable. On the one hand we have the letter which purports to be from Georgiana. I personally have never seen Georgiana's handwriting. I do not know if you, Benham, or you, Graydon, would be prepared to swear that this note is written in her hand?"

Viscount Benham looked worried. "Indeed, Adelaide, I review so many documents and papers that I can only say that this letter does not look dissimilar to others I remember receiving from Georgiana in the past."

Lady Vaudon turned an enquiring glance towards the Marquis. He said curtly, "I have never seen Georgiana's handwriting. There has been no occasion for her to write."

"What we have, therefore," Lady Vaudon said simply, "is a note which may or may not have been written by Georgiana. Even if she has written it, we have no means of knowing whether or not it was written voluntarily."

Viscount Benham said with marked anxiety, "Are you suggesting that Georgiana has been abducted? Such a thing is impossible!"

"I disagree," said the Marquis of Graydon slowly. "Indeed, we should have considered before that Georgiana's fortune represents a temptation that is too great to be ignored." He turned and addressed Lady Vaudon. "It appears that Viscount Benham and I may have allowed ourselves to fall into a somewhat foolish error. If you are correct in believing that Georgiana is an unwilling victim of this supposed elopement, it is obvious that there is a desperate need for haste in tracing her destination. Have you any ideas, ma'am, as to the direction in which I should concentrate my search? Do you think her abductor will try for Gretna Green?"

"We have not yet discussed the other evidence relative to Georgiana's disappearance," Lady Vaudon answered tranquilly. "We have Lady Elizabeth's word for it that Georgiana deliberately contrived to give her the slip in order to arrive at a clandestine assignation. And although Lady Elizabeth unfortunately failed to find Georgiana in time to discover the identity of her male companion, she was *quite* sure that Georgiana accompanied him willingly."

"Very well," said the Viscount irritably, "what are you trying to tell us now? First you convince us that this letter may well be a forgery, then you start telling us that Georgiana left voluntarily after all."

"No," said the Marquis, "that is not what you are trying to say at all, is it, Lady Vaudon? I see that you are telling me to concentrate my search along the routes likely to appeal to Freddie."

"I'm glad to see that you have some brains," said Lady Vaudon calmly.

Viscount Benham expostulated, "Now, now, Adelaide. I cannot have you casting these aspersions on the character of a connection of ours."

"Why not?" asked Lady Vaudon. "You've just finished casting several that are equally bad at Georgiana. Ain't she a connection also? I was under the impression that she was your ward and your goddaughter. Personally, I'd rather lay the scandal at Lady Elizabeth's doorstep any day."

The Marquis drew on his gloves and snatched up his riding crop. "You will forgive me if I leave you to settle this family discussion after my departure!" He turned once more to Lady Vaudon. "I have one further question. Are you in agreement with me that Thayne is the most likely destination? Lady Elizabeth might have suggested to Freddie that it would be safer to head for the Border."

"No," said Lady Vaudon, "she would never tolerate a Gretna marriage for Freddie if it could be avoided. She will certainly try to persuade the Vicar of Thayne to perform the ceremony as soon as she has procured a special licence. I have no doubt that we shall receive word tomorrow morning that Lady Elizabeth has decided to retire to the country in order to recoup her health. She will be hoping that once Georgiana and Frederick are married, my brother will accept the inevitable with as good a grace as possible." She looked searchingly at the Marquis. "You will only have a few hours to find out where they are secreted, you know."

"Never fear, ma'am," responded the Marquis, "I shall put those hours to good use. I bid you goodnight – and thank you!"

"I wish," said Viscount Benham, "that somebody would tell me what this is all about."

"If you sit down and stop scowling," said Lady Vaudon, "I will."

CHAPTER
FIFTEEN

GEORGIANA awoke when they stopped briefly in order to permit four new horses to be harnessed to the carriage. Freddie, revelling in his new role as a man of action, clasped her to his bosom and placed his hand firmly over her mouth, thus effectively preventing her from crying out. She tried biting his hand, but he had had the forethought to wear leather gloves, and her teeth were not strong enough to penetrate the suede. To Freddie's chagrin, she accepted defeat with reasonable equanimity, and instead of pleading with him for mercy, once they were under way again she simply laid her head against the satin squabs and for the second time gave every appearance of dropping off into untroubled slumber.

In reality, such tranquillity was feigned, but Georgiana intuitively sensed that in silence lay her best method of defence. Silence baffled Freddie, leaving him unsettled and uncertain of what manner to adopt. Georgiana, knowing the volatile nature of his emotions, dreading taking any action that might inflame him either to physical violence, or to demonstrations of his supposed affection.

When they arrived at their final destination, therefore, Georgiana was tired and nervous but not exhausted. Freddie, on the other hand, was feeling the inevitable reaction consequent upon achieving a hard-won battle. They had been travelling for almost eight hours, and dawn had long since given way to the clear light of early morning. Georgiana looked around her and saw to her relief that she recognised the countryside, since Freddie had brought her to one of the large farmhouses that formed part of the Thayne estate. Before Lord Thayne had inherited the title, Freddie and his parents had used this house as their country home.

Freddie dismissed the grooms to the stables and crossed the courtyard that separated the carriage from the pleasant stone farmhouse, gesturing to Georgiana that she should follow. He opened the door himself saying, "You need not look for assistance from the servants. Mamma sent somebody down yesterday and had them all taken around to Greenings. She pretended they were needed there to get the house ready for some tenants. Only the outdoor people have been left behind, and they will not venture into the house whatever they may hear."

Georgiana did not deign to reply and sat down on a chair in the entrance hall. "I am tired," she said sharply, "and I feel sick. I wish to retire. I am also hungry," she added with more truth. "Is there nobody to provide us with some refreshment?"

"Mamma has arranged for wine and biscuits to be left in my bedchamber. I will give you some if you come with me."

"Pray do not be foolish, Freddie. You know very well that I cannot possibly accompany you to your bedchamber."

"Well," said Freddie, "you'll have to. I am going to sleep because I am exhausted, and anyway there is nothing for us to do until Mamma gets here. I cannot leave you running around – you would be off before I knew it, and all my trouble bringing you here would be wasted. You will have to go into my dressing-room, and I shall sleep in my bedchamber. There is no window in the dressing-room and no way you can pass out into the corridor except through my room."

He smiled with pleasure. "You see how carefully I have thought it all out? You can rest if you wish, and I can sleep peacefully – and you cannot complain that I am not being a perfect gentleman, although since we are to be married so soon, I really do not see why you are raising so many scruples."

"That is all right," Georgiana said hastily, "I will do as you say and stay in the dressing-room. Please show me where we should go, and let us have a glass of wine together. Then you may rest easily until your mother arrives. Really, there is no point in either of us staying awake – we shall only be bored, after all. As you say, there would be nothing to do except talk to one another."

"Now you are sounding more sensible," approved Freddie contentedly. He reached his bedchamber and threw open the heavy oak door, allowing Georgiana to go before him into the room. "You see that is very comfortable; and you may lock the door of the dressing-room if you wish. So much the better if you prefer to be twice locked in."

As he spoke he drew the heavy bolt across the interior of the bedroom door, grinning with satisfaction at the security of their prison. He offered Georgiana a glass of wine from the decanter standing on one of the tables, and handed her a dish of macaroons that had been covered with a clean white napkin. "Mamma is so clever," said Freddie enviously. "She thinks of everything."

"She does indeed," Georgiana agreed acidly. "Do I have your permission to retire? Every bone in my body is jangling from that coach journey."

"We came at a spanking pace, did we not?" said Freddie proudly. "Ah well, I am sleepy too. If I could only take these dashed boots off, I should be really comfortable. No matter." He flung himself into a deep armchair. "I am too tired to care."

Georgiana watched him intently and silently for several minutes, then slipped quietly into the dressing room, taking the precaution of locking the door after herself. As Freddie had said, there was no window in the room, and consequently it was dark and stuffy. She was amazed at how difficult she found it to keep herself awake, despite the absolute necessity of fighting off the waves of slumber. She hoped fervently that Freddie was feeling similarly afflicted.

At the end of an eternity of time that reason told her might actually be as short as an hour, she quietly turned the key in the dressing-room door and stepped out into the bedroom. Her cousin remained where she had left him, stretched out in the deep armchair, one booted foot resting on a padded stool. Silently she crossed half the room and stood looking at him. He did not move. She bent down and removed her golden evening slippers. The thin leather soles made almost no sound, but stockings would make even less.

On tip-toe she reached the outer door of the bedchamber and stood staring at the heavy bolt with mingled fear and hostility. Finally she shrugged her shoulders. She had very little to lose even if Freddie chanced to wake up and see her. With trembling fingers she eased the bolt along. A slight creak seemed to her heightened senses to sound louder than the trumpet call at judgment. At last the bolt was drawn back and she pulled the door gently open, offering fervent prayers that the servants would have kept the hinges oiled. The door opened soundlessly, and Georgiana blessed Lady Elizabeth and her iron control of the various households under her command.

Outside the door she debated swiftly whether or not to turn the key and thus lock Freddie safely inside. Crossing her fingers, she twisted the key and then pocketed it for good measure.

Swiftly she ran down the stairs, through the empty hall and out of the front door. She had no idea whether the grooms who had travelled down with them understood the nature of Freddie's plans, nor could she know where their sympathies would lie if she once appealed to them for help. However, necessity proved a great aid in forcing swift decisions and Georgiana paused, intending only to re-tie the strings of her shoes before seeking aid from the stablehands. The noise of a galloping horse arriving in the courtyard paralysed her fingers with momentary fright. Her shoe dropped from her hands and she sat down suddenly on a convenient tree-stump, dreading the arrival of Lady Elizabeth just when her escape seemed certain.

"Do you always take off your shoes and lose them when somebody tries to kidnap you?" asked the Marquis of Graydon with cool interest.

Georgiana tried unsuccessfully to hide her stockinged feet beneath the golden hem of her evening gown. "Do you always have to spring out on young ladies just when they are trying to recover their spirits after an emotionally harrowing experience?"

"What have you done with poor Freddie?" asked the Marquis.

"I've locked him in his bedchamber," said Georgiana, "I was just going round to the stables to get a horse."

"Am I never going to be allowed to show you what a useful sort of fellow I am? If a man cannot be allowed to rescue his betrothed from the hands of a villainous abductor because she insists on doing everything by herself, then how is he ever to prove himself worthy of her affections?"

"I do not quite know," responded Georgiana. "Perhaps – if you should happen to be talking about me and not merely discussing the problem in the abstract – perhaps you might consider that I may not wish you to be worthy . . . only loving."

"Georgiana!" The Marquis sprang down from his horse, his face pale with exhaustion and his forehead still damp with sweat. "Georgiana, I seem to have made the most shocking mess of everything so far, and now I am too tired to think of any of the pretty speeches I had prepared for you." He shrugged ruefully. "You must know that I love you," he said, "would you please do me the honour of becoming my wife?"

"I think that was a pretty speech," said Georgiana.

The Marquis placed a firm hand beneath her chin and tipped her face up towards his own. "I have a vivid memory of the last time I kissed you," he said. "I am hopeful that this time your reaction may be a little . . . warmer."

"I shall do my best," whispered Georgiana.

Her highly satisfactory endeavour to show a proper

warmth of affection might have continued for a considerable period of time had the peace of the courtyard not been once more disturbed. The rattle of coach wheels and the clopping of horses' hoofs, however, finally penetrated the romantic haze surrounding Georgiana and the Marquis. Georgiana pressed herself more closely within the protective circle of her betrothed's embrace and said worriedly, "Oh, Julian, it is my aunt!" The Marquis squeezed her gently and turned just in time to bow ironically to Lady Elizabeth as she descended from the coach.

"You!" exclaimed Lady Elizabeth. "What are *you* doing here?"

"It seems to me," replied the Marquis, "that I should be asking you that question."

Lady Elizabeth thought swiftly and with visible effort. "I received a message from the servants here at Redlands that some crisis had developed. I came to investigate."

"Really?" murmured the Marquis. "How . . . er . . . enterprising of you, after the alarms of your expedition to Vauxhall last night. We all thought you quite prostrate after your unfortunate and mysterious illness."

Lady Elizabeth's eyes scanned the courtyard.

"If you are looking for Freddie," Georgiana said helpfully, "I think you may discover him asleep in his bedchamber. He found the journey here rather exhausting."

Lady Elizabeth looked bitterly at her niece. "I do not doubt it," she said.

The Marquis spoke abruptly.

"It is time for us to stop all prevarication, Lady Elizabeth. I do not think we have anything further that we need to discuss, except to make purely practical arrangements for Georgiana's immediate comfort and well-being." He spoke curtly to one of the footmen standing silently beside Lady Elizabeth's carriage. "Please call some grooms round from the stables and arrange for the care of these animals. My horse requires immediate and careful attention – he has been ridden hard and long." He turned back to Lady Elizabeth. "No doubt you will wish to offer Georgiana some refreshment while I make whatever arrangements I can for our return to London. We must not delay further in informing Viscount Benham that his ward has been found."

Georgiana allowed a slightly hysterical giggle to escape. "I think too much haste will not be necessary. I see such a cavalcade arriving as could only belong to Lady Vaudon. However did you all know where to come?"

The Marquis looked challengingly at Lady Elizabeth before smiling at Georgiana. "That was quite easy to discover, my love. We guessed that Freddie would try to hide you somewhere near Thayne, and your progress along the highway was not at all hard to trace. A coach and four horses galloping through the night does not pass by completely unnoticed, you know. And once you approached the neighbourhood of this house, there were several farm labourers working in the fields who were happy to tell me that young Master Thayne's travelling chaise had been seen passing this way. Lady Vaudon is naturally quite capable of following the same trail as myself."

"I see," said Georgiana. "Poor Freddie! He was so proud of his scheme."

"Well," allowed the Marquis, "an abduction is not

such an easy thing to manage. I have heard that there are many pitfalls for unwary kidnappers."

"Indeed, my lord?" said Georgiana primly. "I wonder where you may have heard such matters discussed?"

"My name is Julian," said the Marquis, "and if you are very good I will tell you all about my adventures as a kidnapper one day."

A minor commotion, hardly greater than would be caused by a small earthquake, reverberated throughout the courtyard. Lady Vaudon, resplendent in a travelling cape of magenta velvet, descended from her carriage and was succeeded by Viscount Benham, wearily dismounting from a horse. "Georgiana," he said, "thank God you are safe." He sank down upon the bench. "I am too old for this sort of thing, Georgiana. You will have to hurry up and marry the Marquis, whether he's wound up his business affairs or not. Then he can spend *his* nights chasing you round the countryside rescuing you from your relatives, and I shan't have to follow! I am going back to Vienna. I only have to deal with the Frenchies over there."

Lady Vaudon looked round her with interest. She raised a lorgnette to one languid eye. "Why is Freddie up there banging on that window?" she asked curiously.

Lady Elizabeth emitted a strangled gasp. "Oh my poor son!" Furiously she turned on Georgiana. "I wash my hands of you. I have tried my best, but there is nothing to be done with a niece as ungrateful as yourself. I suppose Freddie is locked in." She looked with loathing at Georgiana and the Marquis, who were trying without notable success to control their laughter.

"You two," she said, "undoubtedly deserve each other."

Lady Vaudon examined them placidly. "Indeed," she observed, "I think they do."

Don't miss these exciting Masquerades!

Masquerade
HISTORICAL ROMANCES

Suspense...mystery...intrigue...history
but most of all...love

Let MASQUERADE historical romances take
you places you've never been, eras you've
only imagined...Elizabethan England,
Napoleonic France, Renaissance Italy,
and many more.

Take a journey into the past and
thrill to the joys and sorrows of
people in love in times gone by.

It will be a journey you'll never forget.